ON AN OD

GERALD KERSH was born in Teddington in 1911. He left school and took on a series of jobs—salesman, baker, fish-and-chips cook, nightclub bouncer, freelance newspaper reporter—and at the same time was writing his first two novels. His career began inauspiciously with the release of his first novel, *Jews Without Jehovah*, published when Kersh was 23: the book was withdrawn after only 80 copies had sold when Kersh's relatives brought a libel suit against him and his publisher. He gained notice with his third novel, *Night and the City* (1938) and for the next thirty years published numerous novels and short story collections, including the comic masterpiece *Fowlers End* (1957), which some critics, including Harlan Ellison, believe to be his best.

Kersh fought in the Second World War as a member of the Coldstream Guards before being discharged in 1943 after having both his legs broken in a bombing raid. He traveled widely before moving to the United States and becoming an American citizen, because "the Welfare State and confiscatory taxation make it impossible to work [in Great Britain], if you're a writer."

Kersh was a larger than life figure, a big, heavy-set man with piercing black eyes and a fierce black beard, which led him to describe himself proudly as "villainous-looking." His obituary recounts some of his eccentricities, such as tearing telephone books in two, uncapping beer bottles with his fingernails, bending dimes with his teeth, and ordering strange meals, like "anchovies and figs doused in brandy" for breakfast. Kersh lived the last several years of his life in the mountain community of Cragsmoor, in New York, and died at age 57 in 1968 of cancer of the throat.

By Gerald Kersh

NOVELS

Jews Without Jehovah
Men Are So Ardent
Night and the City
The Nine Lives of Bill Nelson
They Die with Their Boots Clean
Brain and Ten Fingers
The Dead Look On
Faces in a Dusty Picture
The Weak and the Strong
An Ape, a Dog and a Serpent
Sergeant Nelson of the Guards
The Song of the Flea
The Thousand Deaths of Mr. Small
Prelude to a Certain Midnight
The Great Wash*
Fowlers End*
The Implacable Hunter
A Long Cool Day in Hell
The Angel and the Cuckoo
Brock

STORY COLLECTIONS

I Got References
The Horrible Dummy and Other Stories
Clean, Bright and Slightly Oiled
Neither Man nor Dog: Short Stories*
Sad Road to the Sea
Clock Without Hands*
The Brighton Monster and Other Stories
The Brazen Bull
Guttersnipe
Men Without Bones
On an Odd Note*
The Ugly Face of Love and Other Stories
More Than Once Upon a Time
The Hospitality of Miss Tolliver
Nightshade and Damnations*

* Available from Valancourt Books

ON AN ODD NOTE

BY

GERALD KERSH

With a new introduction by
NICK MAMATAS

VALANCOURT BOOKS

On an Odd Note by Gerald Kersh
First published as a paperback original by Ballantine Books, 1958
First Valancourt Books edition 2015

Copyright © 1958 by Gerald Kersh, renewed 1986 by Florence Kersh
Introduction © 2015 by Nick Mamatas

Published by Valancourt Books, Richmond, Virginia
http://www.valancourtbooks.com

All rights reserved. The use of any part of this publication reproduced, transmitted in any form or by any means, electronic, mechanical, photocopying, recording, or otherwise, or stored in a retrieval system, without prior written consent of the publisher, constitutes an infringement of the copyright law.

All Valancourt Books publications are printed on acid free paper that meets all ANSI standards for archival quality paper.

ISBN 978-1-939140-09-8 (*trade paper*)
Also available as an electronic book.

Cover illustration by Lorenzo Princi/lorenzoprinci.com
Set in Dante MT 10.5/12.7

CONTENTS

Introduction • vii
On an Odd Note • 1
Seed of Destruction • 3
Frozen Beauty • 10
Reflections in a Tablespoon • 14
The Crewel Needle • 27
The Sympathetic Souse • 36
The Queen of Pig Island • 43
Prophet Without Honor • 55
The Beggars' Stone • 72
The Brighton Monster • 79
The Extraordinarily Horrible Dummy • 95
Fantasy of a Hunted Man • 100
The Gentleman All in Black • 104
The Eye • 108

INTRODUCTION

The Man Who Was in Every Story, or, The Murdered Darling

Can there be a more ridiculous thing in the world than an introduction to a volume of Gerald Kersh's fiction? There cannot. These are the first pages of *On an Odd Note* and you, reader, have already climbed the summit of the insane. If this book is in your hands, you know of the glory of Kersh's prose, and so nothing I say matters. If this book isn't in your hands then you're not reading about Gerald Kersh, or your hands, right now, and I may as well stop typing.

Gerald Kersh was once famous. Now he's not even obscure. One novel, *Night and the City*, remains fairly widely circulated, and that mostly on the strength of the first of its two film adaptations, which regularly makes various Best Film Noir lists in print and on the Internet. It's a great film, but its greatness comes only from removing virtually everything of Kersh—his humor, his endless asides that lead the reader down primrose paths to the darkest of alleys, his hard-won close knowledge of the sport of wrestling (and the faux techniques of professional wrestling), the self-destructive interiority of his characters—and replacing it with neo-expressionist cinematography.

Gerald Kersh was not a *neo* anything.

I'm writing from Berkeley, California, the home of several nationally famous new-and-used bookstores: none of them have even a single Kersh title on their shelves. The local library has *Night and the City* on DVD, and four anthologies with Kersh stories, most of them about his famed criminal character Karmesin. Nearby San Francisco manages little better; its large library system contains three anthologies that include Kersh stories, the film, and a copy of his prescient novel of global flooding, *The Secret Masters*. The online catalogue had the gall to ask me if I mean "Kerbs Gerald" instead. *Who the hell is Gerald Kerbs?* (As it turns out, it isn't anybody.)

If you're reading these words, none of what I've said so far is new to you. One doesn't even discover Kersh on the shelves of a dusty old bookstore anymore, one must be initiated into Kersh by someone who knows. Perhaps someone who saw the film and then dared the *Night and the City* novel, and from then on was consumed. Maybe someone who is slightly older, and remembers when Kersh was a prolific writer of short stories, or who owns an old book. A copy of *Prelude to a Certain Midnight*—a crime novel about what a Miss Marple type would really be like—was pressed into my hand a few years ago. Members of the cult of Harlan Ellison may find their way into the smaller sub-cult of Kersh, like a Freemason earning through mystic rite the mystic right to wear ever more ridiculous hats.

Yet, once upon a time, Kersh was ubiquitous. The stories in *On an Odd Note* originally appeared in the great slicks: *Esquire, Playboy, Cosmopolitan*, and *The Saturday Evening Post*, and also *Today,* the *Philadelphia Inquirer* magazine. Remember when every major newspaper had its own Sunday magazine supplement? When *Cosmopolitan* ran fiction? "The Extraordinarily Horrible Dummy" was once routinely reprinted. "The Brighton Monster" was called one of the best fantasy time travel stories of all time by encyclopedist Don D'Ammassa. And now, almost nothing remains of Kersh, at least in the United States. He's largely out of print, almost entirely deaccessioned, and rarely discussed. So here we are, then.

One's first instinct is to blame the work. Most of the stories you'll read in this volume have an O. Henry or *Twilight Zone*-style twist. "The Sympathetic Souse" is a fairly weak story because of its twist, but for the most part the work holds up, despite the seeming flaw of the "gotcha" ending. We know this for one simple reason: the stories are worth re-reading. Kersh is a master of the conversational detail, the slow burn, and of the piquant self-insertion. The stories are not about a twist, they are about everything leading up to the twist, including Kersh himself. "Gerald", "Mr. Kersh", and occasionally just an

"I" telling a story about a story he heard once.

Kersh is a great writer because he eschewed the writing advice of Arthur Quiller-Couch: "Whenever you feel an impulse to perpetrate a piece of exceptionally fine writing, obey it—whole-heartedly—and delete it before sending your manuscript to press. *Murder your darlings.*" Kersh never murdered his darlings; he'd kill everything else first. A story seemingly about the discovery of a new species on a distant island ties into the term *grouch bag*—Merriam-Webster will only tell you that a grouch bag is a purse, and nothing of its history or shape—and from there we get a countess, and a giant, and murder, and the stunning social fact that unrelated little people often look alike to those of average height. These stories are all Kersh, all darlings—forget on *an* odd note, these tales are composed completely of nothing but odd notes.

What happened to Kersh is what will happen to all of us: he died. It's a cliché that writing confers a type of immortality, but in truth most writers outlive their books. Kersh kept plugging away until nearly the end, despite declining health, but publishers and readers forget when a writer isn't there to remind them of his existence.

After Kersh's death, there was a sea change in publishing. In the realm of slick fiction, Raymond Carver and his epigones took over the slots once reserved for short stories in *Esquire*, *The Atlantic*, et al. Kersh's stories are thoughtful and often involve people discussing their lives, but then he adds something: events. Events actually occur in Kersh's fiction. We can't have that!

In science fiction, the 1960s and 1970s saw the rise and fall of New Wave, which paved the way for cyberpunk in the 1980s. Kersh's science fiction and fantasy suddenly felt rather quaint, being neither phantasmagorical nor hard-bitten. There was no more room for stories of sophisticated men and women, and those just imitating sophistication, exploring ever-so-fascinating phenomena with a cynical eye.

Ditto crime/mystery fiction, in which the protagonists of new series simply had to be alcoholics with sexual problems—

joy, whimsy, cleverness were all remanded to the cozies. There is plenty of booze and sex in Kersh's work, but for the most part his characters can handle a fifth of whisky. And if they can't, it is the height of moral approbation for a maître d' character to step in and help soothe and maintain the poor poor dear.

But Gerald Kersh is not just another old-fashioned writer. His work remains vibrant and relevant. His lengthy asides on grappling and jujitsu predate and predict the current rage for mixed martial-arts competitions. He nailed a prediction of the end of the Cold War to within five years, and hinted at the geopolitical chaos to come. Kersh unsentimentally wrote about child murderers and gender roles, casual corruption in journalism, the poison of racism, and all the social and cultural issues we're still working over in our fiction and in the great conversation of society. The world is ready for a Kersh revival, but what is to be done?

The stories in *On an Odd Note* often occupy small narrative universes. There are only a few characters in each tale, and sometimes one that seems obscure or marginal ends up becoming key to the story. And so too, in this introduction: there is Kersh, there is me, and there is you. How can Kersh make his comeback? It's up to you. Here's a non-ridiculous suggestion for anyone ridiculous enough to have read so far: you have this book in your hand, so now get a second copy and give it away to someone—like a Seed of Destruction in reverse—to someone who needs to be in our cult.

Nick Mamatas
Berkeley, California

Nick Mamatas has published over one hundred short stories in a variety of genres: horror, crime, science fiction, fantasy, pornography, transgressive, and experimental. His work has variously appeared in anthologies such as *Best American Mystery Stories*, *Lovecraft's Monsters*, and *Caledonia Dreamin'*, Internet magazines such as Tor.com, *ChiZine*, *Lamplight*, and *Mississippi Review*'s online edition, in print in *Asimov's Science Fiction* and *Weird Tales*, and in literary journals including *subTERRAIN* and *Gargoyle*. His novels include the noir *Love is the Law*, the alcoholic zombie novel *The Last Weekend*, and the Lovecraftian whodunit *I Am Providence*.

ON AN ODD NOTE

For Evelyn Licht

SEED OF DESTRUCTION

I always maintained that Mr. Ziska deserved to get on in the world, if only on account of the extraordinary richness of the lies he told. He started as an antiquary and jeweler in a small way of business, buying and selling all kinds of valueless rubbish—cameo brooches, Indian bangles and job lots of semi-precious stones. I used to let him sell me knickknacks for which I had no earthly use, just for the sake of his sales talks, for in Mr. Ziska's stuffy little shop a paste brooch was not simply a paste brooch—it was, as he could always explain, a very special sort of paste brooch. It had been worn by Dr. Crippen's wife; it had been found in the belly of an ostrich; it had fooled an Indian Maharajah. He nearly persuaded me once that a rusty old Spanish knife with a broken point was the fatal knife used by Charlotte Corday when she stabbed Marat in his bath. It was a left-handed knife, he explained. Unique, amazing opportunity, valuable historical relic, dirt cheap, five pounds. No? Four pounds fifteen shillings. No? Four pounds. Not at any price? Pity, pity to see a friend missing such a bargain! Then what about this valuable old meerschaum pipe, bitten through at the mouthpiece? This was the pipe Emile Zola smoked while he was writing *Nana*—look, crumbs of tobacco still stuck at the bottom of the bowl. A literary man should not fail to snap up this sacred relic. To anybody else five pounds; to me, thirty-five shillings. No? Then how about this candlestick? It belonged to Balzac. With this very candlestick he lighted George Sand through the streets when she went to catch her omnibus . . .

So he ran on. He always got me in the end, so that I still possess Lord Byron's eyeglass, Beethoven's paper weight, a rusty spearhead which belonged to Richard the Lion Hearted, and a brass ring marked with the signs of the zodiac and guaranteed to bring good luck. I have never been able to give the things away. He had what they call personal magnetism, that funny little man. As he talked he glared into your eyes and screwed his face into frightful grimaces. He wore an antiquated frock coat which, he once told me, had been the property of Richard Wagner, and never let himself be seen without a pink orchid in his frayed buttonhole. He was irresistible.

It was Mr. Ziska who invented the incredible legend of the Seed of Destruction. He made it up on the spur of the moment. There was something of the artist in Mr. Ziska. He was tired of telling the same old story about how the shoddy little rings and pins that he sold would bring good fortune to the ladies or gentlemen who wore them, and so he struck a new note. He had an inspiration. It came to him in a flash. I was there when it happened.

He had stopped trying to sell me Charles Dickens' favorite gold toothpick, and had taken from a tray a gold ring set with a spinel seal as big as my thumbnail, clumsily engraved with a bit of an inscription in Arabic. He stood there, blinking at it. I could see that he was trying to think of something fresh, and so I said, "The Seal of King Solomon, no doubt?"

He blinked at me and smiled shyly and said, "No, this is not the Seal of Solomon. This, my friend, is known as the Seed of Destruction."

"It brings good luck, I suppose?"

His eyes sparkled and his face assumed such an expression of delight that every wrinkle looked like a little smile, as he replied, "No, my young friend, that is just where you're wrong. It does *not* bring good luck. It brings *bad* luck," and he actually crowed like a contented baby.

He continued, "It brings bad luck. That's why it's called the Seed of Destruction. It brings very bad luck indeed. The inscription says: *The destiny of man is trouble*. If you're rich, it'll make you poor. If you're healthy, it'll make you ill. If you're alive, it will be the cause of your death pretty soon. See? It was cut by a magician, an Arabian magician, a very bad man indeed, for an Arab prince in the days of Saladin. The magician put a spell on it, a shocking spell. This ring is absolutely certain to bring bad luck. Not good luck—bad luck. I personally guarantee it. A bargain, twenty-five pounds."

"And you expect me to pay twenty-five pounds for that?" I said. "And, incidentally, it does not seem to have done *you* much harm. Come off it, Mr. Ziska!"

With infinite patience and something like pity, holding up his hand for silence, he said, "Calm, calm, calm! Listen and learn, young man. I have not told you how the enchantment works. This ring does no harm at all to the purchaser of it. Not to the buyer, and not to the seller. I bought it and therefore it cannot hurt me. If you buy it, it cannot hurt you. But if you *give* this ring away, the most horrible misfortunes will fall upon the head of the person to whom you give it. Do you understand? That is the whole idea of the thing. It is obvious, can't you see? The Arab prince fell in love with a princess, but she loved another prince instead of him. Do you see? So the prince paid the magician a lot of money to make this ring and, pretending brotherly affection, he placed it on his rival's finger. Three days later, the rival was eaten by a lion. But the princess, poor girl; she went to bed and died of a broken heart. And so the prince, who was sorry for what he had done, got the ring and hid it away. But one of the eunuchs of his palace stole it."

"What happened to him?" I asked, knowing that Ziska was lying.

"Oh, it is equally unlucky to steal it. It must be bought and paid for. The eunuch was set upon by robbers and they cut his throat and stole the ring from him and sold it to a merchant in Aleppo. But they hadn't paid for it, so they were caught and had their heads cut off. But the merchant sold the ring to a young nobleman so *he* was all right. He had bought and paid for it. The nobleman, who was trying to keep on the right side of his uncle who was very miserly and wicked, gave him the ring for a present. And would you believe it? That same day, the wicked old uncle fell off a high roof and broke his neck and the young nobleman inherited all his money. I could go on all day telling you what happened. Twenty-five pounds?"

"I haven't got any rich uncles and I haven't got an enemy worth killing. And I haven't got twenty-five pounds."

"Perhaps you think I'm not telling you the truth?" said Ziska.

"No, no!" I protested.

"Yes, I can see. You think I'm a liar. You're as good as calling me a liar to my face. That's what it is, and I treat you like a friend. I want to do you a good turn and sell you the famous Seed of Destruction for twenty-five pounds, and you as good as call me a swindler, a confidence trickster, a cheat! Very well."

"No, no, my dear Mr. Ziska. Don't take it like that."

In order to mollify him I had to buy a cracked china inkpot—the one Shakespeare used when he was writing *Hamlet*.

Later I heard that Mr. Ziska had sold the Seed of Destruction to a passionate-looking thin lady who ground her teeth between sentences and had dark circles under her eyes, which were swollen with weeping. He asked fifty pounds for the ring and got it. It was a fair price. The ring was worth four or five, and the story, as he later elaborated it, was reasonably cheap at forty-five pounds or so.

I congratulated Mr. Ziska and forgot about the affair until I was reminded of it by a sensational feature article in a Sunday paper. It was entitled "Jewels of Death," and was composed of a little fact and a lot of fiction about famous unlucky gems. We have all read that sort of thing before. The article was illustrated with photographs of the Great Blue Diamond, the Bloody Ruby of Cawnpore, the Peruvian Emerald and, last of all, the Seed of Destruction. This strange spinel seal, it appeared, had a sinister history. Mr. Ziska's story was there, more or less as I had heard it when he concocted it in his shop.

The writer went on to say that the Seed of Destruction had been discovered by the ill-fated Mrs. Mace in an obscure and nameless little cheap jewelry shop. Mrs. Mace, believing in the mysterious virtue of this terrible gem, had given the ring to her faithless lover, who was surprised by her jealous husband two days later and beaten to death with a sculptor's mallet. Mrs. Mace, who appeared to be somewhat demented, had told the story in court. She had sold the Seed of Destruction to a morbidly curious City business man, who, having given her his word of honor that he would never give the ring away without receiving payment for it, gave it to his partner, with a friendly slap on the back one afternoon in Sweetings.

Less than an hour after he had put the ring on his finger, the hapless partner of the City business man was run over and instantly killed by a heavy truck in Cheapside. It is true that he was under the influence of drink when staggering off the curb, but it looked very peculiar, one had to admit. He had never been run over before.

The ring, together with his other effects, went to his heir, a worthless young man, who squandered everything, forged seven checks, was sent to prison, and died there of pneumonia.

The pawnbroker, who by this time had the Seed of Destruction as an unredeemed pledge, made much of the fact. An American bought it for a considerable sum, and added it to his collection of horrible curios. A burglar stole the collection, was stopped by a policeman, and pulled a gun. The thief shot the policeman in the shoulder, but the policeman shot him in the abdomen so that he perished miserably a few hours later, and the ring went back to the man who had bought it. One evening, however, his daughter, who had been drinking bathtub gin with some friends, took the ring out of her father's private museum, and put it on in sheer drunken bravado. She defied the Seed of Destruction, said the writer of the article.

The party went on. Dawn broke and the daughter, although she could hardly stand, insisted on taking out a high-powered roadster. She said she needed a breath of fresh air. She zigzagged at seventy miles an hour along the highway, miscalculated on a hairpin bend and crashed. That was the end of her.

The bereaved father sold the Seed of Destruction for one cent to a millionaire from Detroit and embraced the Catholic religion.

And now once again the Seed of Destruction was on the market. The depression had struck America, and the millionaire from Detroit, in straitened circumstances, had sold his collection of jewels to Tortilla, the dealer, who was waiting to see how much he could get for the Seed of Destruction, which I could have bought for twenty-five pounds that day in Ziska's shop.

More than two years later, as I was whistling to a taxi in Piccadilly outside the place where they sell dog-collars, an extremely elegant young man stopped me and said, "Excuse me, you're Mr. Kersh, aren't you?"

I said that I was indeed.

"I don't think you remember me," he said.

I said, "My memory is getting very bad. As a matter of fact, I don't think I do remember you."

"Does the name of Ziska convey anything to you?" he asked. "My name is Ziska. I saw you in my father's shop."

I said, "Why, of course it does. Surely you must be old man Ziska's son?"

We shook hands. A taxi came and we shared it. I asked young Mr. Ziska how his father was. He sighed and said, "I have taken over the business. But I'll never be anything like he was. What a man he was! What a personality! What a business man! But of course, you know, in our business we have to have good eyes. A jeweler who can't see straight might as well retire. Dad was marvelous. But about five years ago his poor old eyes gave out on him. He got a cataract, had an operation, and he was never the same again. I took over. What a man he was! I dare say you remember that funny business about the Seed of Destruction?"

"I know," I said, "because I happened to be on the spot when your father made it up!"

Young Mr. Ziska said, "Yes, I know. I wish I had a half of the old man's imagination. *I* can't do it. He could spin you a story about anything. I have known him to sell six pennorth of pinchbeck for ten pounds just on the strength of the story he made up about it on the spur of the moment. Well, as I was saying, it was his story that made that Seed of Destruction what it is today. He bought it for fifty shillings and sold it for fifty pounds. And now—I can speak to you freely because you're an old friend—it must be worth fifty thousand pounds if it's worth a penny. I've been offered four thousand pounds for it."

"Oh, have you got it then?" I asked.

"Yes, I bought it off Tortilla for three thousand pounds. I knew I could get four thousand pounds for it anyway, so I bought it. Who wouldn't? I knew it would please the old man. He was a great guy. I wanted to give him a little surprise so I brought this Seed of Destruction home and said to him, 'You'll never guess what I've got.' Then he asked me what I had got and I told him and he was as pleased as punch. He was pretty sick, and getting on in years, as I dare say you know. I said to him, 'Well, here you are, Dad, you invented it, you made it, you built it up, you worked miracles with it; you picked a tuppenny-halfpenny spinel out of a boot-box full of rubbish and turned it into a property by your own genius, and here it is—worth a packet. I make you a present of it,' I said. And then he asked me how much I had paid for it, and I told him three thousand pounds, and he sat up in bed with the ring on his little finger and he shouted 'Oi!' and passed away. Heart failure. Shock. It had cost him fifty shillings. He was a great guy. Where are we, Shaftesbury Avenue? I get out here. Nice to have seen you again. Bye-bye."

FROZEN BEAUTY

Do I believe this story?

I don't know. I heard it from a Russian doctor of medicine. He swears that there are certain facets of the case which—wildly unbelievable though it sounds—have given him many midnight hours of thought that led nowhere.

"It is impossible," he said, "in the light of scientific knowledge. But that is still a very uncertain light. We know little of life and death and the something we call the Soul. Even of sleep we know nothing.

"I am tired of thinking about this mad story. It happened in the Belt of Eternal Frost.

"The Belt of Eternal Frost is in Siberia.

"It has been cold, desperately cold, since the beginning of things . . . a freak of climate.

"Did you know that a good deal of the world's ivory comes from there? Mammoth ivory—the tusks of prehistoric hairy elephants ten thousand years dead.

"Sometimes men digging there unearth bodies of mammoths in a perfect state of preservation, fresh enough to eat after a hundred centuries in the everlasting refrigerator of the frost.

"Only recently, just before Hitler's invasion, Soviet scientists found, under the snow, a stable complete with horses—standing frozen stiff—horses of a forgotten tribe that perished there in the days of the mammoths.

"There were people there before the dawn of history; but the snow swallowed them. This much science knows. But as for what I am going to tell you, only God knows. . . ."

I have no space to describe how the good doctor, in 1919, got lost in the Belt of Eternal Frost. Out of favor with the Bolsheviks, he made a crazy journey across Siberia toward Canada. In a kind of sheltered valley in that hideous hell of ice, he found a hut.

". . . I knocked. A man came; shabby and wild as a bear, but a blond Russian. He let me in. The hut was full of smoke, and hung with traps and the pelts of fur animals.

"On the stove—one sleeps on the brick stove in the Siberian winter—lay a woman, very still. I have never seen a face quite like hers. It was bronze-tinted, and comely, broad and strong. I could not define the racial type of that face. On the cheeks were things that looked like blue tattoo marks, and there were rings in her ears.

"'Is she asleep?' I asked, and my host replied; 'Yes; forever.' 'I am a doctor,' I said; and he answered; 'You are too late.'

"The man betrayed no emotion. Maybe he was mad, with the loneliness of the place? Soon he told me the woman's story. Absolutely simply, he dropped his brief sentences. Here is what he said:

I have lived here all my life. I think I am fifty. I do not like people around me.

About fifteen . . . no, sixteen years ago I made a long journey. I was hunting wolves, to sell their skins. I went very far, seven days' journey. Then there was a storm. I was lucky. I found a big rock, and hid behind it from the wind. I waited all night. Dawn came. I got ready to go.

Then I see something.

The wind and storm have torn up the ground in one place, and I think I see wood. I kick it. I hit it with my ax. It is wood. It breaks. There is a hole.

I make a torch and drop it down. There is no poisonous air. The torch burns. I take my lamp and, with a little prayer, I drop down.

There is a very long hut. It is very cold and dry. I see in the light of my lamp that there are horses. They are all standing there frozen; one with hay or something, perhaps moss, between his teeth. On the floor is a rat, frozen stiff in the act of running. Some great cold must have hit that place all of a sudden—some strange thing, like the cold that suddenly kills elephants that are under the snow forever.

I go on, I am a brave man. But this place makes me afraid.

Next to the stable is a room. There are five men in the room. They have been eating some meat with their hands. But the cold that came stopped them, and they sit—one with his hand nearly in his mouth; another with a knife made of bronze. It must have been a quick, sudden cold, like the Angel of Death passing. On the floor are two dogs, also frozen.

In the next room there is nothing but a heap of furs on the floor, and sitting upon the heap of furs is a little girl, maybe ten years old. She was crying, ever so long ago. There are two round little pieces of ice on her cheeks, and in her hands a doll made of a bone and a piece of old fur. With this she was playing when the Death Cold struck.

I wanted more light. There was a burned stone which was a place for a fire.

I look. I think that in the place where the horses are, there will be fodder. True; there is a kind of brown dried moss. The air is dry in that place! But cold!

I take some of this moss to the stone, and put it there and set light to it. It burns up bright, but with a strong smell. It burns hot. The light comes right through the big hut, for there are no real walls between the rooms.

I look about me. There is nothing worth taking away. Only there is an ax made of bronze. I take that. Also a knife, made of bronze too; not well made, but I put it in my belt.

Back to the room with the furs in it, where the fire is blazing bright. I feel the furs. They are not good enough to take away. There is one fur I have never seen, a sort of gray bear skin, very coarse. The men at the table, I think, must have been once, long ago, strong men and good hunters. They are big—bigger than you or me—with shoulders like Tartar wrestlers. But they cannot move any more.

I stand there and make ready to go. There is something in this place I do not like. It is too strange for me. I know that if there are elephants under the frost, still fresh, then why not people? But elephants are only animals. People, well, people are people.

But as I am turning, ready to go, I see something that makes my heart flutter like a bird in a snare. I am looking, I do not know why, at the little girl.

There is something that makes me sorry to see her all alone there in that room, with no woman to see to her.

All the light and the heat of the fire is on her, and I think I see her open her eyes! But is it the fire that flickers? Her eyes open wider. I am afraid, and run. Then I pause. *If she is alive?* I think. *But no*, I say, *it is the heat that makes her thaw*.

All the same, I go back and look again. I am, perhaps, seeing dreams. But her face moves a little. I take her in my arms, though I am very afraid, and I climb with her out of that place. Not too soon. As I leave, I see the ground bend and fall in. The heat has loosened the ice that held it all together—that hut.

With the little girl under my coat, I go away.

No, I was not dreaming. It is true.

I do not know how. She moves. She is alive. She cries. I give her food; she eats.

That is her, over there, master. She was like my daughter. I taught her to talk, to sew, to cook—everything.

For thousands and thousands of years, you say, she has lain frozen under that snow—and that this is not possible. Perhaps it was a special sort of cold that came. Who knows? One thing I know. I found her down there and took her away. For fifteen years she has been with me—no, sixteen years.

Master, I love her. There is nothing else in the world that I love. She has grown up with me, but now she has returned to sleep.

"That's all," the doctor said.

"No doubt the man was mad. I went away an hour later. Yet I swear—her face was like no face I have ever seen, and I have traveled. Some creatures can live, in a state of suspended animation, frozen for years. No, no, no, it's quite impossible! Yet, somehow, in my heart I believe it!"

REFLECTIONS IN A TABLESPOON

I remembered all this in a grim, cold, Northern restaurant. A sour waiter, twisting his face in a pale sneer, banged down a plateful of something flabby floating in gray water and, snarling over his shoulder, said that I could have Spam or boiled salt cod and brussels sprouts to follow. I replied that in the meantime I needed a spoon, so he brought one, wiped it on his trousers, and let it fall with a clang. Then he went away with a shrug of despair. It was a magnificent tablespoon, weighing several ounces, heavily plated and monogrammed—a relic of old, good, solid days. Turning it over I saw the autograph of Gino engraved on the handle.

Gino's name, scrawled with a flourish, looked remarkably like Gino himself: the big loop and the fine curly tail of the G were the nose and the mustache, the *ino* recklessly sprawling downward were the pendulous lower lip and the three fat chins of that noble restaurateur. His silverware had gone under the hammer, I supposed; and I wondered what had happened to the bold brass fittings and the honest round mirrors that used to look so massive and gay in Gino's Long Bar. Gino, I knew, had turned to dust, which he hated, and to flowers, which he loved—he was always beating away dust or arranging flowers—but his place had been built to last a thousand years. All the same, it began to die when Gino died of an enlarged heart in 1933—I always thought that his heart was dangerously big for a man who owned a restaurant; yes, the place went into a decline and sank from owner to owner until a bomb closed its eyes in 1940. It had been beloved for Gino's sake—he was a good man, bright and kind; people in trouble found their way to Gino as lost dogs find their way to a watchman's fire in the cold, inhospitable night. Things pass: they break, or they wear away . . .

"You don't like?" grunted the waiter, jerking a contemptuous thumb toward my soup. I said, "I see that you have some of poor old Gino's silverware here."

"You knew him?"

"He was my friend," I said, "he gave me credit." The waiter changed. He stood up and grew taller; he smiled and became friendly. He whispered, "In a minute I get you two nice little lamb cutlets." We smiled at each other. I was moved—although Gino was dead and the dust carts had dragged away the rubble that had been his house, by God's grace his generous heart had not stopped beating. The waiter said, "He was patient. My goodness, what would've drove me mad, so it only made M'sieur Gino say *Well!* My Gawd, you remember that yellow woman what she called herself 'The Countess'? With the scar on her face?"

"Gino was very patient with her," I said, "poor woman." The waiter winked and said, "Don't drink that muck; I get you two nice little lamb cutlets—they do you more good, yes?" "Yes," I said and he went away, flapping like a seal on his big flat feet in his shiny black coat.

. . . The Countess had been a beautiful lady, but when I knew her she was nothing but an attenuated shadow in a late afternoon. Her scar, a small one over her left cheekbone, made her face arresting. She was reminiscent of beauty, as an echo is like a voice. Yet in spite of her wild yellow hair, nobody denied that she was a lady. Have you ever come upon a ruin left tottering after an air raid—some bit of bedroom wall, for example, broken beyond repair, still retaining a few strips of carefully chosen wallpaper? You know that although blast has opened it to the rain and that it is pitiful in its exposure, it has in its day been beloved: it has witnessed certain glorious moments. The Countess was such a ruin.

She always had a little money on the first of every month—about eight pounds. Then she was a great lady, ready to carry the weight of all the troubles of the world. For about two days she gave drinks to strangers and money to beggars. On the fifth day she would be alone, twitching, with the Black Dog looking over her shoulder into the small glass which she was trying to keep half-emptied until somebody happened to offer her something. It was awful to see her on the edge of the twenty-one arid deserts of her next three weeks. Then Gino would catch the barman's eye and nod, looking tired and sick. His nod said: *Let her have credit.* He insisted only that she eat something. Sometimes he would coax: "Madame la Comtesse, for you especially I make a little something—not for anybody, not for everybody, but for *you!*" She was always contemptuous, and said, "It doesn't concern me. I am not interested in your little something."

"If I have make it, could Madame la Comtesse not be gracious and say, 'I will taste'?"

"Very well, only you must cash me a check."

"First you must give me your opinion. There is an entrecôte. Nobody could tell, nobody could judge—only you. We beg your opinion." And so she ate. As for her bill, Gino charged it to 'Expenses,' as the saying goes: he chalked it up and washed it out. Knowing this, the Countess grew more and more capricious, intolerably haughty. How could she admit that she was accepting charity? It was out of the question. "Laugh at me, laugh at me now!" she would cry, while her eyes flickered; she could not meet the horrible white stare of the Hangman Sobriety. "Laugh at me, laugh if you like, but I say I could have bought a dozen Ginos a little while ago!" To this, Gino always replied, "Dear lady, there is nothing to buy, nothing at all."

The last time I saw her she was trying to cash a check. "September the what?" she asked, making blots on the dateline of a crumpled blue slip with a miniature fountain pen. A respectable bystander said, "The fourth, madam, September the fourth."

"Of course it's the fourth, I know very well it's the fourth. I didn't need you to tell me that. . . . Gino, you will cash my check for two pounds?" Gino gave her two pounds and, closing her poor smudged checkbook, slipped it back into her bag. She glared at him and screamed, "You thief! How dare you go over my bag?"

Gino murmured, "Be nice, put away your checks. Among friends, one trusts. Away, away—put it away!" He knew that her checks were valueless, they always came back; but she, tossing her bewildered head and still trying to write, said: "The *fourth*?—of what month? Of *September* . . . September the *fourth*. . . ."

I heard Gino mutter, "Oh God, the sea is so wide and the boat is so small!" But then the Countess, waggling her useless checkbook, said with an odious and provocative grin, "I'll tell you something. The Monk Paphnutius looked into my eyes—I was a girl of fourteen then—and he said, 'You shall betray and be betrayed, and be loved by one whom you do not love and give your love to one who does not love you! You shall avenge your own victim, and after that you shall order the destiny of an Oriental Empire!' . . . You and your dirty two pounds—"

The bar was filling. Gino said, "Dear lady, you are always welcome, but since you are excited you had better go and rest a little." On the verge of tears she exclaimed, "And a little while ago I could have employed this creature to brush my shoes, and he would have been honored!" But she walked out, pushing the revolving door so violently that it thudded fifteen times. A few seconds later we heard a woman's scream, a screeching of brakes, and a smashing clangor of metal and glass. Everybody looked at everybody else. The door revolved again, very slowly, and the Countess came back trembling, with a pale face. "It just missed me," she said.

The chasseur, following her, said that she had missed death by inches, having stepped off the pavement in front of a speeding car which, swerving in order not to hit her, had skidded across the street into some railings. The Countess was ordering a drink. Gino, shaking his head at the barman said, "No, dear lady, this is all—no more. Just one last drink with me, for your nerves, and then God bless you! You must not come here any more." She wept: "The Monk Paphnutius looked into my eyes . . . and I, who rule an Oriental Empire, that *I* should be spoken to like this, oh . . . oh . . ." Gino nodded and said, "Yes, Madame la Comtesse, even you, good-bye for God's sake.

You have an Empire, I have a License—enough is enough!" She went away, trailing her old-fashioned handbag, and Gino said, "Monks! Eyes! Empires! Licenses! I wish to God Almighty that I was an American sitting on a flagpole."

I never saw the Countess again . . .

The waiter came back with the cutlets. They were burned on the outside and raw within. He was unconcerned. While a man at an adjacent table stamped his feet and beat hideous noises out of a crust with his knife handle, the waiter talked of Gino and of what a man he had been.

"Except somebody sometimes he liked everybody always," he said. Then the manager came and almost dragged him away.

. . . I knew one of the men whom Gino did not like: a ruffian out of the Balkans, a man with a withered arm, who always had something to sell—a silk handkerchief, for example, with somebody else's monogram or a fountain pen, fine today, oblique tomorrow, marked with any name but his own. He answered to the name of Stavro, and he was an unscrupulous villain, an unmitigated blackguard, and a swindler by vocation. His right arm and hand were bent into something like the shape of a tired rattlesnake. This deformity appeared to be the result of some recent injury, for the first time I saw him, in the spring of the year of Gino's death, the arm was caught up in a black silk sling and he had the drawn look of a man suffering persistent pain. Even so, he was handsome in a dark, pantherish way; one sensed the man's power over women and hoped that God would have mercy upon any infatuated creature that fell into his grip, for Stavro would have no mercy at all.

I never saw a stonier pair of bright black eyes. He was short but beautifully proportioned, a sort of vest-pocket Hercules, unquestionably a dangerous man in a rough-house for all his fastidiousness of dress and manner, and his gentleness of voice. For no definable reason I also detested him; with Gino it was hate at first sight. Stavro had a disconcerting way of looking at you—he gazed right into your eyes with the hungry, immovable, wide-eyed stare of a pervert or a watching cat. He seemed to be having trouble with a match and a cigarette, so I offered him a light. He thanked me graciously and said, "This is nothing, this arm. I am almost ambidexterous. I can write with my left hand, even. Look—" He took out a fat green fountain pen, unscrewed the cap with the help of his fine white teeth, and scribbled *Stavro* on the marble-topped table "—Do you like my pen?" he asked.

"It is very nice."

"You can have it for two pounds if you like. It cost me three guineas." He was lying, of course; he was not the man to pay good money for anything. I wondered what he did for a living and concluded that he got a risky livelihood on the fringe of the underworld, buying things on credit and selling them quickly for cash, walking off with other people's luggage . . . always moving quickly and quietly, elusive, a Disappearing Man in a conjuring trick, here today, gone tomorrow; best left alone. Later Gino said, "I am an old man and you are a young man. Allow me to warn you; keep away from that dark one. He is no good, he is a pomp." He meant "pimp" and was not far wrong at that.

Stavro went on talking, purring out self-glorification: "My left hand is as good as my right. I will show you something. There are not many men *you* know can do this—" He whisked an elegant pearl-and-silver fruit knife out of a waistcoat pocket, opened it with two fingers and his teeth, turned his head and pointed to a small wooden sign two yards away, which advertised somebody's Highland Whisky in elegant gold lettering. "Which do you prefer? The dot over the *i* in *Highland* or in *Whisky?*" I did not know what he meant. He explained, "I will dot you the *i* in Highland." Then, with a casual snap of his powerful fingers he flicked the little knife away. The point buried itself in the center of the dot he had specified. "Have I earned a drink?" he asked, retrieving his knife and putting it away. I said that he had, indeed, and I bought him one. In the end I bought his fountain pen.

Stavro frequented Gino's Long Bar for several weeks. His arm, free from the sling, was permanently distorted, fixed in its peculiar, weary, reptilian droop. He told me that all the tendons and muscles had been cut to pieces so that he would never use that arm again. He hooked himself on to me, and to others also. I was not sorry when Gino told him to go and stay away. "No," he said one morning, as Stavro came in, "you are not coming here any more. Get out and keep out; I don't want you in my bar . . . Why? . . . Because I don't like your face in the first place, and in the second place *you* are keeping *nice* people away. Go, please." Stavro, smiling with his mouth while he murdered Gino with his eyes, bowed and walked out. It is odd that, thinking of Gino, I should think of the only two customers whom I saw sent away from the genial and kindly atmosphere of his bar. Mourning Gino, I remember his enemies. It is strange.

. . . As I have said, I never saw the Countess again, but I did meet Stavro once, nearly twelve years later. He had changed, so that I was almost sorry for him. Although he was still elegantly dressed and carried himself, as always, like a gentleman, he had got fat. All his feline litheness, all his supple charm, were dead and buried under an extra hundred pounds of flesh. I recognized him first by his right arm, which was still withered and useless, and then by his eyes, which were still bright and wicked. He, with his swindler's memory, remembered me immediately, and greeted me as if we had parted only a day or two before. He asked me how the fountain pen was working. I had given it away ten years ago, cursing myself for having been hypnotized into buying it. I told him so and he laughed, and then we went to a nearby wine bar for a glass of sherry.

I looked at Stavro in a mirror, as Perseus looked at the evil face of the Gorgon, and it occurred to me that while some great men may die with their best songs unsung, this fat crook was destined to go to the grave with most of his evil unconsummated. This idea filled me with a strange sense of peace; I knew, then, that while there is certainly a Devil, there is unquestionably a God. I said to Stavro, "Can you do with a couple of pounds?" He looked at me, stunned with astonishment. "Do I understand that you are offering me money?" he asked. "Without rancor, as man to man," I said. He was touched. He took the money, bought me a drink with one of the notes, and put the change in his pocket. Then he said, "I accept your money in the spirit in which it is offered. I love frankness, openness, and candor between man and man." He was a born liar. He went on: "And for this two pounds I will give you something worth two thousand. I will tell you the story of *myself*." Stavro looked at me with expectancy, and made a protective gesture with his good hand, as if he feared that I might be thunderstruck and utterly overwhelmed by his magnanimity. But, observing that I bore up, he plunged straight into the great drainpipe of his past.

He had been a very bad man indeed, worse than I could have guessed. Among other things, he had been a professional killer, an assassin employed by one of the political murder associations of the Balkans. I know that the man was a liar, yet what he said rang true; I remembered, for example, the terrifying little trick by means of which he had first aroused my interest, that trick with the knife. He was not, he told me, one of the directors of political assassination; he was an operator, an agent. He might work, for example, with a few underlings; he might, perhaps, train and arm a boy like Princip, the crazed student who fired the shot that started the first World War. Stavro had nothing to do with Princip, but he was involved in similar affairs. Several gentlemen (never heard of in Western Europe) big names in the Balkans, met their deaths through Stavro. In important cases he, Stavro in person, with his deadly right eye and terrible right hand, dealt with the killing.

He was one of those men who have the knack of pointing a gun as you or I point a finger. He never missed. As for his nerves, he had none. It was not that he was fearless; he lacked the capacity to feel fear, just as he was incapable of understanding the meaning of pity. If it was necessary to torture somebody, Stavro would torture him, quite dispassionately. He was not a sadist; he found no pleasure in inflicting pain—it was all a matter of business, as far as he was concerned. I believe that in telling me all this he had in mind some rakeoff from a fat fee such as the Sunday newspapers were paying for stories like his own. He became explanatory, almost eloquent. With a passionless wink he told me that he knew perfectly well how nothing was any good without a love interest; and if I wanted love interests, good Lord, he could embarrass me with the richness of his love-life: he was Cupid, the indiscriminate gunman.

He said, "There is, though I say so who should not, my dear friend, something in me to which women are—or have been—drawn, I tell you, as iron is drawn to a magnet. I was known as irresistible. Why? I will tell you why. With women, it is pretty much the same as with hunting wild animals; more often than not they run away a little ahead of the noise you make while approaching. Irritate them, and—in the case of fierce, proud animals—they will charge you in order to destroy you; and then, if you are a man with a clear eye, a cool head, and perfect confidence in yourself, the animal that charges you delivers itself into your hands. In other cases, for example shy and bewildered creatures, it is necessary to gain a certain advantage . . . to creep up, having calculated the wind. But that is neither here nor there.

"My successes have nearly always been with the wild, fierce ones: there is infinitely more satisfaction as your Shakespeare says in rousing a lion than in starting a hare. 'The blood more stirs,' I think he said. I am a big-game hunter—irritate, stimulate; wound if necessary; arouse interest; then out of the undergrowth comes your animal, with slashing claws and foam at the mouth. Poor wretch! Little does it know that *I* am here with a thunderbolt, quite unafraid, almost sorry for it. Then . . . *Bang!*—a rug for my study. For example, there was in a certain city a woman who was known as 'The Golden'—gold hair, gold skin, gold eyes, and as good as gold. I will tell you details . . ." And Stavro told me details.

The lady to whom he referred was a famous beauty who had come out of a good family to marry into an illustrious one. She was the toast of her country, and her husband, the well-born and noble gentleman who adored her, was regarded as a fortunate man, since she remained unspoiled. The Emperor Franz-Josef had tried to lead her astray; her virtue was impregnable.

Stavro, however, managed to assail that virtue. In the case of 'The Golden' it must have been the nostalgia for the mud, such as affects certain women from time to time. However it happened, Stavro succeeded. There was a hideous scandal. The lady's husband blew his brains out. She had committed only social suicide, and lived on. She was ostracized; she went away, lived a gay life, ran through most of her money, lost the residue in the war, and went to the dogs. It was a nasty story.

"Good, eh?" said Stavro. I made no reply; I could feel again in my nostrils the sulphurous bite of smoldering Evil that goes on and on and ends God knows where. Stavro continued: "I tell you all these things because I regard you as my personal friend. You don't know what you have done for me in lending me this money—" He touched his waistcoat pocket. "Tomorrow is a bad day in my life. Tomorrow is my birthday. All my troubles began on my birthday—I was born; if I had not been born I should never have had any troubles. On my fourteenth birthday I was punished by my father for something I never did. On my sixteenth I did something and was found out. On my eighteenth, after a certain incident, I had to leave home. On my twentieth I went to prison, and escaped a death sentence by the skin of my teeth. On my twenty-first birthday I did an important job for Zedoff, risking my neck and getting two bullets in the shoulder, and I never got paid because Zedoff, losing his nerve, ran away to America.

"All my life misfortune has followed me and has caught up with me invariably on my birthday; that is, tomorrow. And if I can, when the calendar tells me that it is here, I spend my birthday in a quiet place, in retirement. Your two pounds will enable me to do this: I shall go to a village near London and spend my birthday in bed. No harm has ever come to *me* in bed. What does your Bible say? 'Cursed be the day . . .' et cetera? Cursed be the day, cursed be the night . . . I am not a literary man. This arm, this good right arm, this piece of dead wood which I must carry with me to my grave—I got this on my birthday too. And here, by the way, my dear friend, is another little incident which might provide food for your satirical humor and material for your penetrating pen. (I am sorry, by the way, about that pen I sold you, and I will get you another, even cheaper and much better.)

"I knew it, I knew that if I started important business on my birthday I should come to grief. But there was no way out of it. I was under orders from Marko. It was, I may say, a big job, and I will give you the details of it later if you think you can use them. You have done me a favor and I will do one for you, and we will split fifty-fifty. It is true that you write it down, but without—for example, *me*!—what would there be for you to write about? Do you realize, my dear friend, that *I*, the man you see before you, I, Stavro—*I* was the man delegated to kill a dictator? I will not insult you by asking whether you have heard of Mustapha Kemal Pasha, the Gray Wolf. God only knows what that man has survived. If I were religious I should say that God had chosen him, that God is keeping him for some kind of destiny, since he is the only man who, given to *me* for killing, is not yet dead. There was big money in it too. If I told you that my own share, after everything had been weighed and paid, was to be thirty thousand pounds, perhaps you would call me a liar? Yet this is the case, I give you my word of honor.

"Marko had organized it. Kemal had to be at a certain place at a certain time, and when he got there, a certain gentleman (not a hundred miles from here) was to put a bullet out of a Mannlicher sporting rifle into him—a semi-hollow, soft-nosed bullet. And there was a crowd, actually and positively a *multitude* of reliable men hired and ready to cover my retreat. I tell you that there are fates, as your Shakespeare has it, destinies that have us in their power whatever we may do. Is it 'Rough-hew our ends?' or 'Shape them as we will?' I am no poet.

"It was all organized; organized, *cher ami*, so as to be foolproof—it couldn't possibly fail. I may say that with *me* gripping that rifle, with *my* eye looking along that barrel, Kemal was as good as dead. And I as good as had thirty thousand pounds in the bank; I mean, in the Safe Deposit, because I don't use banks. All I had to do was catch the boat train from Victoria, and I left half an hour earlier in order to make assurance doubly sure. As I left my hotel I realized that it was my birthday, and fear came upon me. You know what I mean when I say fear.

"I told the driver to drive with infinite care. He did, and a tire blew out. By the time we were ready to start again, a little time had passed and it was necessary to hurry. And then, taking a shortcut round Charing Cross and rushing through an absolutely empty street—what happened? Ha!

"Some drunken woman steps off the pavement, my driver spins his wheel, we hit the railings of the church across the road, I put up my hand to save my eyes and the shock of the impact sends it through a window; the glass cuts my arm into a fine fringe, and I am in hospital for two months. I lose my thirty thousand pounds; Mustapha Kemal lives; and I am a cripple! . . . There, for example, is my birthday luck for you."

I said, "If your birthday is tomorrow, that makes it September the fourth, doesn't it?"

Stavro nodded and replied, *"Too* true."

I bought him another drink. "Did you ever hear of the Monk Paphnutius?" I asked.

His eyes narrowed. "What makes you ask?"

I said, "Nothing. And as a matter of curiosity, my dear Stavro, did the lady known as 'The Golden' have a little scar on her face?"

Stavro, tense as a hungry cat and watching me closely, said, "On her left cheek. What then?"

I answered, "Nothing, nothing . . ."

The waiter, having dealt with his impatient customer, came back with a deplorably soggy portion of pie and, lingering, said, "And that other one, that one with the funny arm. Eh? M'sieur Gino, he didn't like that one. And look what happened to him, eh?"

"Stavro?"

"That's it, Stavro."

"What happened to him, then?"

"It was in the papers. The police was after this man with

this funny arm, this Stavro. So he goes to Waterloo Station. So he buys a ticket to Walton-on-Thames. So he puts down a pound-note. So it is a *bad* pound-note. A counterfeit, a forgery. So one thing leads to another—see?—so in the end, so he runs away, and—*bomp!* Right! into a motorcar. *Smash-bang!* . . . no more Stavro. Last thing he says is, 'So *this* is my birthday?' "

"Ha," I said. "Bad? A *bad* pound?"

"Yes, on his birthday. Coffee, sir?"

"No, no coffee. On his birthday, eh?" Before I paid the bill I held a pound-note up to the light. "Will you look the other way while I steal Gino's spoon?" I asked.

"Take! I give!" said the waiter, looking sideways to be certain that the manager's back was turned. "What is it? You see something?"

"I never passed a bad note before," I said. "Keep the change." The waiter laughed and I, having shaken hands with him, went to catch my train.

THE CREWEL NEEDLE

Certain others I know, in my position, sir, have had "severe nervous breakdowns"—gone out of their minds—took to parading the streets with banners, and what not, shouting *Unfair!* Well, thank God, I was always steady minded. I could always see the other side of things. So, although I really was unjustly dismissed from the force, I could still keep my balance. I could see the reason for the injustice behind my dismissal, and could get around to blaming myself for not keeping my silly mouth shut.

Actually, you know, I wasn't really sacked. I was told that if I wanted to keep what there was of my pension, I had better resign on grounds of ill health. So I did, and serve me right. I should never have made my statement without first having my evidence corroborated. However, no bitterness—that ends badly, mark my words. Justifiable or unjustifiable, bitterness leads to prejudice which, carried far enough, is the same thing as madness. . . . I started life in the Army, d'you see, where you learn to digest a bit of injustice here and there; because if you don't it gets you down and you go doolally.

If I had been thirty years wiser, thirty years ago, I might have been retired, now, on an inspector's pension. Only, in the matter of an open verdict, I didn't have the sense to say nothing. I was young and foolish, d'you see, and therefore over-eager. There was a girl I was very keen on and I was anxious to better myself—d'you see?

I was supposed to be an intelligent officer, as far as that goes in the police force. But that isn't quite good enough. In those days all the so-called intelligence in the world wouldn't get a policeman very far—seniority aside—unless he had a kind of spectacular way of showing it.

I'm not embittered, mind you. Nothing against the force.

Only I ought to have known when to stop.

At first, like everybody else, I thought nothing of. it. The police were called in after the doctor, merely as a matter of routine, d'you see. I was on a beat, then, in Hammersmith. Toward about eight o'clock one Sunday morning, neighbors on either side of a little house in Spindleberry Road were disturbed by the hysterical crying of a child at Number Nine.

At first there was some talk of the N.S.P.C.C., but there was no question of that, because the people at Number Nine were, simply, a little orphan girl, aged eight, and her aunt, Miss Pantile, who thought the world of her niece and, far from ill-treating the child, had a tendency to spoil her; because the little girl, whose name was Titania, was delicate, having had rheumatic fever.

As is not uncommon, the houses in Spindleberry Road are numbered odd coming up, and even going down. The neighbors in question, therefore, were Numbers Seven and Eleven. Spindleberry Road, like so many of them put up around Brook Green before the turn of the century, is simply a double row of brick barracks, sort of sectionalized and numbered. Under each number, a porch. In front of each porch, iron railings and an iron gate. At the back of each house, a bit of garden: they are accessible from front or back only.

Beg pardon—I've never quite lost the habit of making everything I say a kind of report. . . . Well, hearing child crying, neighbors knock at door. No answer. Number Seven shouts through letter-box, "Open the door and let us in, Titania!" Child keeps on crying. Various neighbors try windows, but every window is locked from the inside. At last, Number Eleven, a retired captain of the mercantile marine, in the presence of witnesses, bursts in the back door. Meanwhile, one of the lady neighbors has come to get a policeman, and has found me at the corner of Rowan Road. I appear on the scene.

Not to bother you, sir, with the formalities; being within my rights, as I see them in this case, I go in, having whistled for another policeman who happens to be my sergeant. The house is in no way disturbed, but all the time, upstairs, this child is screaming as if she is being murdered, over and over again: "Auntie Lily's dead! Auntie Lily's dead!"

The bedroom is locked on the inside. Sergeant and I force the lock, and there comes out at us a terrified little golden-headed girl, frightened out of her wits. The woman from Number Eleven soothes her as best she can, but the sergeant and I concentrate our attention upon Miss Lily Pantile, who is lying on a bed with her eyes and mouth wide open, stone dead.

The local doctor was called, of course, and he said that, as far as he could tell, this poor old maiden lady had died of something like a cerebral hemorrhage at about three o'clock in the morning. On a superficial examination this was as far as he cared to commit himself. He suggested that this was a matter for the coroner.

And that, as far as everybody was concerned, was that, d'you see. Only it was not. At the inquest it appeared that poor Miss Pantile had met her death through a most unusual injury. A gold-eyed crewel needle had been driven through her skull, and into her brain, about three inches above the left ear!

Now here, if you like, was a mystery with a capital M.

Miss Pantile lived alone with her eight-year-old niece. She had enough money of her own to support them both, but sometimes made a little extra by crewel work—you know, embroidering with silks on a canvas background. She was especially good at creweling roses for cushion covers. The needle she favored—she had packets and packets of them—was the Cumberland Crewel Gold Eye, one of which had found its way, nobody knew how, through her skull and into her brain. But how?—that was the question.

There was no lack of conjecture, you may be sure. Doctors cited dozens of instances of women—tailoresses and dressmakers, particularly—who had suddenly fallen dead through having needles embedded in various vital organs. Involuntary muscular contractions, it was demonstrated, could easily send an accidentally stuck in needle, or portion of a needle, working its way between the muscles for extraordinary distances, until it reached, for example, the heart. . . .

The coroner was inclined to accept this as a solution, and declare a verdict of death by misadventure. Only the doctor wouldn't have that. Such cases, he said, had come to his attention, especially in the East End of London; and, in every case, the needle extracted had been in a certain way corroded, or calcified, as the case might be. In the case of Miss Lily Pantile, the crewel needle—upon the evidence of a noted pathologist—had been driven into the skull *from the outside*, with superhuman force. Part of the gold eye of the needle had been found protruding from the deceased's scalp. . . . What did the coroner make of that? the doctor asked.

The coroner was not anxious to make anything of it.

In the opinion of the doctor, could an able-bodied man have driven a needle through a human skull with his fingers?

Definitely, no.

Might this needle, then, have been driven into Miss Pantile's skull with some instrument, such as a hammer?

Possibly; but only by someone of "preternatural skill" in the use of instruments of exceptional delicacy. . . .

The doctor reminded the coroner that even experienced needlewomen frequently broke far heavier needles than this gold-headed crewel needle, working with cloth of close texture. The human skull, the doctor said—calling the coroner, with his forensic experience, to witness—was a most remarkably difficult thing to penetrate, even with a specially designed instrument like a trephine.

The coroner said that one had, however, *to admit the possibility* of a crewel needle being driven through a middle-aged woman's skull with a hammer, in the hands of a highly skilled man.

. . . So it went on, d'you see. The doctor lost his temper and invited anyone to produce an engraver, say, or cabinet-maker, to drive a crewel needle through a human skull with a hammer "with such consummate dexterity"—they were his words, sir—as to leave the needle unbroken, and the surrounding skin unmarked, as was the case with Miss Pantile.

There, d'you see, the coroner had him. He said, in substance:

"You have proved that this needle could not have found its way into the late Miss Pantile's brain from inside. You have also proved that this needle could not have found its way into Miss Pantile's brain from outside."

Reprimanding somebody for laughing, then, he declared an open verdict.

So the case was closed. A verdict is a verdict, but coroners are only coroners, even though they may be backed by the Home Office pathologist. And somehow or other, for me, this verdict was not good enough. If I had been that coroner, I thought to myself, I would have made it: Willful murder by a person, or persons, unknown.

All fine and large. But what person, or what persons, known or unknown, with specialized skill enough to get into a sealed house, and into a locked room; hammer a fine needle into a lady's skull, and get out again, locking all the doors behind him, or them, from the inside—all without waking up an eight-year-old girl by the side of the victim?

Furthermore there was the question of motive. Robbery? Nothing in the house had been touched. The old lady had nothing worth stealing. Revenge? Most unlikely: she had no friends and no enemies—lived secluded with her little niece, doing no harm to anyone. . . . You see, there was a certain amount of sense in the coroner's verdict . . . Still . . .

"Only let me solve this mystery, and I'm made," I said to myself.

I solved it, and I broke myself.

*

Now, as you must know, when you are in doubt you had better first examine yourself.

People get into a sloppy habit of mind. I once read a detective story called "The Invisible Man," in which everybody swore he had seen nobody; yet there were footprints in the snow. "Nobody," of course, was the postman, in this story; "invisible" simply because nobody ever bothers to consider a postman as a person.

I was quite sure that in the mystery of Miss Pantile there *must* have been something somebody overlooked. Not a clue, in the generally accepted sense of the term, but *something*.

And I was convinced that somehow, out of the corner of my mind's eye, I had seen in Miss Pantile's bedroom, a certain something-or-other that was familiar to me, yet very much out of place. Nothing bad in itself—but in the circumstances, definitely queer. Now what was it?

I racked my brains—Lord, but I racked my silly brains!—trying to visualize in detail the scene of that bedroom. I was pretty observant as a youngster—I tell you, I might have got to be detective-inspector if I'd had the sense to keep my mouth shut at the right time—and the scene came back into my mind quite clearly.

There was the room, about sixteen feet by fourteen. Main articles of furniture, a pair of little bedsteads with frames of stained oak; crewel-worked quilts. Everything neat as a pin. A little dressing-table, blue crockery with a pattern of pink roses. Wallpaper, white with a pattern of red roses. A little fire-screen, black, crewel-worked again with yellow roses and green leaves. Over the fireplace, on the mantel-shelf, several ornaments—one kewpie doll with a ribbon round its waist, one china cat with a ribbon round its neck, half a pair of cheap gift-vases with a paper rose stuck in it, and a pink velvet pincushion. At the end of the mantel-shelf nearest the little girl's side of the room, several books—

". . . Ah-ah! Hold hard, there!" my memory said to me. "You're getting hot!" . . . You remember the old game of Hot-and-Cold, I dare say, in which you have to find some hidden object? When you're close to it you're hot; when you're not, you're cold. When my memory said "Hot," I stopped at the mental image of those books, and all of a sudden the solution to the Spindleberry Road mystery struck me like a blow between the eyes.

And here, in my excitement, I made my big mistake. I wanted, d'you see, to get the credit, and the promotion, that would certainly come with it.

Being due for a weekend's leave, I put on my civilian suit and went down to Luton, where the orphan girl Titania was staying in the care of some distant cousin, and by making myself pleasant I got to talking with the kid alone, in a tea-shop.

She got through six meringues before we were done talking. . . .

She was a pale-faced little girl, sort of pathetic in the reach-me-down black full mourning they'd dressed her in. One of those surprised-looking little girls with round eyes; mouth always part open. Bewildered, never quite sure whether to come or to go, to laugh or to cry. Devil of a nuisance to an officer on duty: he always thinks they've lost their way, or want to be taken across a street.

Her only truly distinguishing mark or characteristic was her hair, which was abundant and very pretty. Picture one of those great big yellow chrysanthemums combed back and tied with a bit of black ribbon.

I asked her was she happy in her new home? She said, "Oh yes. Auntie Edith says as soon as it's decent I can go to the pictures twice a week."

"Didn't your Auntie Lily let you go to the pictures, then?" I asked.

Titania said, "Oh no. Auntie Lily wouldn't go because picture houses are dangerous. They get burned down."

"Ah, she was a nervous lady, your Auntie Lily, wasn't she," I said, "keeping the house all locked up like that at night?"

"She was afraid of boys," Titania said, in an old-fashioned way. "These boys! What with throwing stones and letting off fireworks, they can burn you alive in your bed."

"That's what your poor Auntie said, isn't it, Titania? Now, you're not afraid of boys, are you?"

"Oh no," she said. "Brian was a boy. He was my brother."

"What, did Brian die, my little dear?" I asked.

"Oh yes," she said. "He died of the flu, when Mummy did. I had the flu, too. But *I* didn't die; only I was delicate afterwards. I had the rheumatic fever, too."

"Your brother Brian must have been a fine big boy," I said.

"Now about how old would he have been when he passed away? Twelve?"

"Thirteen and a quarter," said Titania. "He was teaching me how to spit."

"And so he passed away, and I'm very sorry to hear it," I said. ". . . And your Auntie Lily wouldn't let you go to the pictures, wouldn't she? Well, you must always obey your elders, as you are told in the catechism. Who did you like best in the pictures?"

Her face sort of lit up, then, d'you see. She told me: "Best of all I liked Pearl White in a serial, *Peg O' The Ring*. Oh, it was good! And John Bunny and Flora Finch—" She giggled at the memory. "But we had only got to Part Three of *The Clutching Hand* when Mummy and Brian died, and I went to live with Auntie Lily. . . . Apart from the danger of fire, picture palaces are unhealthy because they are full of microbes. Microbes carry germs. . . . Auntie Lily used to wear an influenza mask on her face when she went out—you know, you can't be too careful these days," said this serious little girl.

"And kept all her windows locked up, too, I daresay," I said. "But I mean to say, what did you do with yourself? Play with dolls?"

"Sometimes. Or, sometimes, I did sewing, or read books."

"Ah, you're a great one for reading, Titania," I said, "like your poor mother used to be. Why, Titania is a name out of a fairy story, isn't it? A clever girl like you could read anything she could get her hands on, if she were locked up with nobody to talk to. I bet you read your poor brother's old books, too. I remember noticing on the mantel-piece a bound volume of the *Boy's Own Paper*. And also . . . now let me see . . . a book with a black and yellow cover entitled *One Thousand Things a Clever Boy Can Do*—is that it?"

She said: "Not *Things*! *Tricks*."

"And right you are! *One Thousand Tricks a Clever Boy Can Do*. And I'll bet you mastered them all, didn't you?"

She said, "Not all of them. I didn't have the right things to do most of them with—"

"There's one trick in that book, which I have read myself," I said, "which you did master, though, and which you did have the right apparatus for, Titania, my dear. Tell you what it is. You get a medium needle and stick it down the center of a soft cork. Then you get a penny and place this penny between two little blocks of wood. Put your cork with the needle in it on top of the penny, and strike the cork a sharp blow with a hammer. The cork will hold the needle straight, so that it goes right through that penny. That's the way you killed your poor Auntie Lily, isn't it, Titania?"

Finishing the last of her meringue, she nodded. Having swallowed, she said, "Yes," and, to my horror, she giggled.

"Why, then," I said, "you must come back to London with me, d'you see, and tell my inspector all about it."

"Yes," she said, nodding. "Only you mustn't tell Auntie Edith."

I told her, "Nobody will do anything dreadful to you; only you must confess and get it off your poor little mind."

Titania's second cousin Edith, by courtesy called "Auntie," came with the child and me to London . . . and there, in the police station, she flatly denied every word of everything, and cried to be sent home.

Put yourself in my position, stigmatized as a madman and a brute! I lost my temper, one word led to another, and I "tendered my resignation. . . ."

I shall never forget the sly expression on the girl Titania's face when she went back with her Auntie Edith to Luton.

I have no idea what has happened to her since. She will be about thirty-eight or thirty-nine by now, and I should not be at all surprised if she had turned out to be quite a handful.

THE SYMPATHETIC SOUSE

The Carpathians have always been the rocky-breasted wet nurse of somber and terrible fantasy. Dracula came out of these parts in which, as the peasants whisper, crossing themselves: "The dead ride hard." Hungary, and Austria, have always been breeding grounds for vampires, werewolves, witches, warlocks, together with their bedevilments and bewitchings.

Psychoanalysis started in these parts. There are hundreds of professional psychologists (witch-doctors) from most other countries in the world who have studied under Freud, Jung, Adler, Groddeck, and the rest. Most of them go away with unblinking conviction: a species of owl stuffed with conjecture curdled into dogma. It is interesting, by the way, to observe that most of these fumblers in the dark are in a state of permanent nervous breakdown—an occupational disease you get when you try to take someone else's soul to pieces and clean it and reassemble it. No man in the world ever emptied his heart and mind in an analyst's office or anywhere else—only madmen try, who do not know what they are talking about; their candor is fantasy.

Anglo-Saxons ought to leave psychology to take care of itself. They break their hearts trying to make an exact science of what—considering the infinite permutations and combinations of the human mind—can never crystallize out of mere philosophy. In the end it all boils down to repetitive case-histories, reports, and other rubbish—sex in statistical tedium, with the spicy bits veiled in the obscurity of a dead language.

So, in effect, said that shrewd little mental specialist whom I will call Dr. Almuna, when I met him in a select scientific group at a cocktail party. He runs the Almuna Clinic—a polite, expensive kind of looney bin not far from Chicago—and specializes in dope-fiends and alcoholics.

Almuna is good company. This cheerful man who has kept clean because he has learned how to wash his hands in any kind of water—this Almuna, a kindly cynic, believes everything and nothing. There is nothing didactic about Dr. Almuna: he admits that the more he knows he knows, the less he knows he knows.

Once, in the course of a conversation he said to me, in reply to a certain question, "I know the lobes of a brain, and have followed the convolutions of many brains, and the patterns of behavior of many men and women. And still I cannot pretend to understand. I try, believe me! But every human brain is a separate labyrinth. He would be a lucky man who, in a lifetime, got to the heart of anybody's brain. No, no; quite simply, I do not try to explain. I treat, and endeavor to understand. The other way lies theory. Hence, fanaticism; and so delusion. . . ."

On the occasion to which I have referred, when earnest professional men made a group and discussed cases, Dr. Almuna was there, cocking his head like a parrot; one eye shut; avidly attentive. Some practitioner whose name I forget was talking of a case of "sympathetic pains." He had investigated and thoroughly authenticated the case of a girl who, at three o'clock in the morning of January 7th, 1944, uttered a piercing shriek and cried, "I'm shot!" She pointed to a spot under the collar-bone. There, mysteriously, had appeared a small blue dot, exquisitely painful to the touch. It transpired that exactly at that moment her brother, who was serving overseas, had been struck by a bullet in that very place.

Dr. Almuna nodded, and said, "Oh, indeed, yes. Such cases are not without precedent, doctor. But I think I can tell you of an even more extraordinary instance of physical sympathy between two brothers. . . ."

Smiling over his cigar, he went on:

. . . These two brothers, let us call them John and William, they came to me at my clinic in Vienna, in the spring of 1934, before Mr. Hitler made it imperative that I leave for foreign parts—even Chicago!

John came with his brother William. It was a plain case, open and shut, of dipsomania. Aha, but not so plain! Because there was such a sympathy between these brothers, William and John, that the weakness of the one affected the other.

William drank at least two bottles of brandy every day. John was a teetotaller—the very odor of alcohol was revolting to him. William smoked fifteen strong cigars a day. John detested the smell of tobacco smoke—it made him sick

Yet account for this, if you like, gentlemen—William, the drunkard and the smoker, was a harmless kind of fellow, while his brother John, the total abstainer, the non-smoker, showed every symptom of chronic alcoholism, cirrhosis of the liver, and a certain fluttering of the heart that comes of nicotine poisoning!

I do not suppose that any doctor has had the good luck to have such a case in his hands. There was William, breathing brandy and puffing cigar smoke like a steam engine, in the pink of condition; blissfully semi-comatose; happy. And there was John, with a strawberry nose, a face like a strawberry soufflé, eyes like poached eggs in pools of blood, fingers playing mysterious arpeggios all over the place—a clear case of alcoholic polyneurotic psychosis—but John had never touched a drop.

It was John who did most of the talking—the one with the strawberry nose. He said, "Dr. Almuna, for God's sake, stop him! He's killing me. He's killing himself, and he's killing me."

William said, "Pay no attention, doc. John's a man of nerves. Me, I take things easy."

At this John cried, "Nerves! Damn you, William, you've torn mine to shreds!"

William said, quite placidly, "Give me some brandy, doctor."

And then you would have been amazed to see the play of expression on the face of John, the plaintive one. He folded his hands and gripped them tight to stop the tremor; and I have never seen a more remarkable combination of desire and revulsion in a human countenance.

"Don't!" he said; and then: ". . . Well, doctor, if you think it's okay . . ."

Alas that I should say it—to an inquiring mind, however well-disposed, all men are guinea pigs. Besides, it might be argued, who was John to say what the suave and comfortable William might, or might not, have? Experimentally, if you like, I gave William three ounces of brandy in a measured glass. It went down like a thimbleful, and he smiled at me—a smile that was pleasant to see.

And believe me or believe me not, his brother John began to retch and hiccup and blink at me with eyes out of focus, while William, having lit a strong cigar, folded his hands on his stomach and puffed smoke!

Sympathy, what? Wow, but with a vengeance!

At last, after a fit of deep coughing, and something like nausea, brother John said, "You see, doctor? Do you see? This is what I have to put up with. William won't let me work. Do you appreciate that? He won't let me work!"

Both John and William were evidently men of substance. They had arrived in a custom-built Mercedes-Benz, were tailored by Stolz, and carried expensive jewelry. It is true that William was covered with cigar-ash, and that his platinum watch had stopped in the afternoon of the previous day; but it was impossible not to detect a certain air of financial independence.

John, the strawberry-faced, the tremulous one, he was neat as a pin, prim, dapper. I wish I knew the laundress who got up his linen. He wore a watchchain of gold and platinum and on the little finger of his left hand a gold ring set with a large diamond. There was about two carats of diamond, also, stuck in his black satin tie. . . .

How shall I describe to you this weird mixture of dandyism and unkemptness in John? It was as if someone had disturbed him in the middle of a careful toilet. His clothes were beautifully cut and carefully pressed. You might have seen your face in the mirrors of his shoes. But his hair needed trimming—it came up at the neck in little feathers—and his fingernails were not very tidy. William was flagrantly, cheerfully—I may even say atavistically—dirty, so as to be an offense to the eye and to the nostrils. Still, he too wore well-cut clothes, and jewelry:

not diamonds; emeralds. Only rich men can afford to be so elegant or so slovenly.

So I asked, "Work, Mr. John? Come now, what do you mean by 'work'?"

William, rosy and contented, was smiling and nodding in a half-sleep—the picture of health and well-being. And his brother John, who had not touched a drop, was in a state of that feverish animation which comes before the sodden sleep that leads to the black hangover.

He said, "Oh, I don't *need* to work—I mean, not in point of economy. Mother left us enough, and much more than enough. Don't you worry about your fee, doctor—"

"You leave Mother out of this," said William. "Little rat. Always picking on Mother, poor old girl. Give us another bit of brandy, doctor; this is a bore."

Before I could stop him William got hold of the bottle and swallowed a quarter of a pint. He was very strong in the hands, and I had to exert myself to take the bottle away from him. After I had locked it up, it was—believe me!—it was poor John who said, in a halting voice, "I think I am going to be sick." What time William, blissfully chewing the nauseous stump of a dead cigar, was humming *O Doña Clara*, or some such trash.

And upon my soul, gentlemen, John joined in, in spite of himself, making what is politely called "harmony":

> *O Doña Clara,*
> *Ich hab' dich tanzen gesehn,*
> *Und deine Schoenheit*
> *Hat mich toll gemacht . . .*

Then John stopped, and began to cry.

He said, "That's all he knows, you see? You see what he is? A pig, a vulgar beast. My tastes are purely classical. I adore Bach, I love Mozart, I worship Beethoven. William won't let me play them. He breaks my records. I can't stop him. He's stronger in the hands than I am—exercised them more. Day and night he likes to bang hot jazz out of the piano; and he won't let me think, he won't let me work—doctor, he's killing me! What am I to do?"

William lit another green cigar and said, "Ah, cut it out, will you? ... Why, doc, the other day this one ordered in a record by a guy called Stravinsky, or something." He chuckled. "It said on the label, *Unbreakable*. But I bust it over his head, didn't I, Johnny? Me, I like something with a bit of life in it ... rhythm. You know?"

John sobbed. "My hobby is painting miniatures on ivory. William won't let me. He mixes up my paints—"

"Can't stand the smell of 'em," said William.

"—Jogs my arm and, if I protest, he hits me. When I want to play music, he wants to go to sleep. Oh, but if *I* want to sleep and *he* wants to make a noise, try and stop him!"

"Let's have a little more brandy," said William.

But I said to him, solemnly, "The stuff is deadly poison to you, Mr. William. I strongly urge that you spend about three months in my sanatorium."

"I won't go," he said. "Nothing the matter with me. *I'm* okay."

"Make him go, *make* him go!" his brother screamed. "Oh William, William, for God's sake—for *my* sake—go to the sanatorium!"

"I'm okay," said William, cheerfully. "You're the one that needs the sanatorium. I'm not going. I'd rather stay at home and enjoy myself. A short life and a merry one. Ha?"

And the extraordinary fact of the matter was, William was, as he said, okay—liver impalpable, kidneys sound, heart in excellent condition—he, who drank two quarts of brandy every day of his life! A tongue like a baby's, eyes like stars, steady as a rock. It was John who showed the stigmata of the alcoholic and the cigar-fiend—he who had never tasted liquor or tobacco.

How do you like that for sympathy?

John whispered brokenly, "I might have tried to bear it all; only last week this sot proposed marriage to our housekeeper! Marriage! To our housekeeper! I can't bear it, I can't bear it!"

William said, "Why not? Nice woman. Johnny hates her, doc, but she understands me. Past her prime, maybe, but comfortable to be with. Shares my tastes. Likes cheerful music. Don't say no to a highball. Cooks the way I like it—plenty of pepper, rich stuff with a lot of spice. This Johnny-boy, here, all he can take is milk and boiled weakfish. Yes, so help me, I'm going to marry Clara. . . . Sure you can't let me have another little bit of brandy, doc? An itsy-boo?"

I said, "No. For the last time, are you sure that you won't come to my sanatorium?"

"Sure as you're sitting there," said William, while John sobbed helplessly on the sofa.

So, to conclude: The brothers John and William went out to where their great limousine was waiting in the dusk, and drove away.

Shortly afterward, John died in delirium of cirrhosis, nephritis, dropsy, and "the whole works"—as you put it. His brother William died soon after, and they were buried together in the Sacred Heart cemetery.

Curious, what?

The good Dr. Almuna rubbed his hands and chuckled.

A listening psychiatrist said, "Most extraordinary," and began an explanation that promised to be interminable.

But Dr. Almuna cut him short. He said, "The explanation, my dear doctor, is an exceedingly simple one. Perhaps I failed to mention that John and William were Siamese twins, and had only one liver between them. And poor John had the thin end of it, which cirrhosed in advance of William's."

He added: "Intriguing, what? Perhaps the only case on record of a man drinking his teetotal brother to death."

THE QUEEN OF PIG ISLAND

The story of the Baroness von Wagner that came to its sordid and bloody end after she, with certain others, had tried to make an earthly paradise on a desert island, was so fantastic that if it had not first been published as news, even the editors of the sensational crime magazines would have thought twice before publishing it.

Yet the von Wagner Case is commonplace, considered in relation to the Case of the Skeletons on Porcosito, or "Pig Island," as it is commonly called.

The bones in themselves are component parts of a nightmare. Their history, as it was found, written on mutilated paper in Lalouette's waterproof grouch bag is such that no one has yet dared to print it, although it happens to be true.

In case you are unacquainted with the old slang of the road, a *grouch bag* is a little pouch that used to hang about the necks of circus performers. It held their savings, and was tied with a gathered string, like the old-fashioned dorothy bag. This was necessary because circus-encampments used to be hotbeds of petty larceny. So on the high trapeze the double-back-somersault man wore his grouch bag. The lion tamer in the cage of the big cats might forget his whip or lose his nerve; he would never forget or lose his grouch bag, out of which would be filched the little moist roll of paper money that was all he had to show for his constantly imperiled life.

Lalouette carried her grouch bag long after the gulls had picked her clean. It contained sixty-seven hundred dollars and a wad of paper with a scribbled story, which I propose to make public here.

It is at once the most terrible and the most pathetic story I have ever had to tell.

At first the ship's captain who landed on Porcosito, who subscribed to a popular science magazine, thought he had discovered the Missing Link—the creature that was neither man nor ape. The first skeleton he found had a subhuman appearance. The thorax was capacious enough to contain a small barrel; the arms were remarkably long and the legs little and crooked. The bones of the hands, the feet and the jaw were prodigiously strong and thick. But then, not far away—it is only a little island—in a clump of bushes, he found another skeleton of a man who, when he was alive, could not have been more than two feet tall.

There were other bones: bones of pigs, birds and fishes; and also the scattered bones of another man who must have been no taller than the other little man. These bones were smashed to pieces and strewn over an area of several square yards. Wildly excited, happy as a schoolboy reading a mystery story, the captain (his name was Oxford) went deeper, into the more sheltered part of Porcosito, where a high hump of rock rises in the form of a hog's back and shelters a little hollow place from the wind that blows off the sea. There he found the ruins of a crude hut.

The roof, which must have been made of grass or light canes, had disappeared. The birds had come in and pecked clean the white bones of a woman. Most of her hair was still there, caught in a crack into which the wind had blown it or the draft had pulled it. It was long and fair hair. The leather grouch bag, which had hung about her neck, was lying on the floor in the region of the lower vertebrae, which were scattered like thrown dice. This human skeleton had no arms and no legs. Captain Oxford had the four sets of bones packed into separate boxes, and wrote in his log a minute account of his exploration of the tiny island of Porcosito. He believed that he had discovered something unexplainable.

He was disappointed.

The underwriters of Lloyds, in London, had with their usual punctiliousness paid the many thousands of pounds for which the steamship *Anna Maria* had been insured, after she went down near Pig Island, as sailors called the place. The *Anna Maria* had gone down with all hands in a hurricane. The captain, officers, passengers, cargo and crew had been written off as lost. Faragut's Circus was on board, traveling to Mexico.

Captain Oxford had not found the remains of an unclassified species of overgrown, undergrown and limbless monsters. He had found the bones of Gargantua the Horror, Tick and Tack the Tiny Twins, and Lalouette.

She had been born without arms and legs, and she was the Queen of Pig Island. It was Lalouette who wrote the story I am telling now. . . .

Tick and Tack were tiny, but they were not twins. A casual observer sees only the littleness of midgets, so that they all look alike.

Tick was born in England and his real name was Greaves. Tack, who was born in Dijon, Brittany, was the son of a poor innkeeper named Kerouaille. They were about twenty-five inches tall, but well-formed, and remarkably agile, so that they made an attractive dancing team. They were newcomers to the circus, and I never saw them.

But I have seen Gargantua and Lalouette; and so have hundreds of thousands of my readers. Gargantua the Horror has haunted many women's dreams. He was, indeed, half as strong and twice as ugly as a gorilla. A gorilla is not ugly according to the gorilla standard of beauty; Gargantua was ugly by any reckoning. He did not look like a man, and he did not quite resemble an ape. He was afflicted by that curious disease of the pituitary gland which the endocrinologists term acromegaly. There is a well-known wrestler who has it.

Something goes wrong with one of the glands of internal secretion, so that the growth of the bones runs out of control. It can happen to anyone. It could happen to me, or to you; and it produces a really terrifying ugliness. Gargantua, as it happened, was by nature a man of terrible strength. George Walsh has told me that he might have been heavyweight weight-lifting champion of the world. An astute promoter realized that there was money in his hideousness; so Percy Robinson rechristened himself Gargantua the Horror, grew a beard—which came out in tufts like paint brushes all over his face—and became a wrestler. As a wrestler he was too sweet-natured and silly, so he drifted into a side show. Naked to the waist, wearing only a bearskin loincloth, he performed frightening feats of strength.

In a fair in Italy I saw him lift on his back a platform upon which a fat man sat playing a grand piano. That same evening I saw Lalouette. I would not have seen her if I had not been in the company of a beautiful and capricious woman who said, when I told her I had a prejudice against going to stare at freaks, that if I would not come with her she would go in alone. So I bought the tickets and we went into the booth.

Lalouette was an aristocrat among freaks. She drew great crowds. Having been born without arms and legs she had cultivated her lips and teeth, and the muscles of her neck, back and stomach so that she could dress herself, wash herself, and, holding a brush or pencil in her lips, paint a pretty little picture in watercolors or write a letter in clear round longhand. They called her Lalouette because she could sing like a bird.

One had the impression that she could do anything but comb her hair. She could even move a little, by throwing her weight forward and sideways in a strange rolling motion. Lalouette painted a little picture while we watched and sang a little song, and my lady friend and I, overcome with admiration and with pity agreed that a woman of her accomplishment might have been one of the greatest women in Europe if the Lord in his wisdom had seen fit to make her whole. For she was a lady, superbly educated, and extremely beautiful—a blonde with great black eyes and magnificent hair of white-gold. But there she was, a freak on a turntable: nothing but a body and a head, weighing fifty pounds.

I had some conversation with her. She spoke five languages with perfect fluency and had read many books. Inquiring into her history I learned that she came of a noble, ancient, overbred Viennese family. Indeed, royal blood ran in her veins, and some fortune-teller had told her mother the countess that the child to which she was about to give birth would be a ruler, a queen.

But when the child was born they saw a monstrosity. The count fainted. The countess loved Lalouette and cherished her, devoted her wretched life to the unfortunate girl who, soon after she could speak, demonstrated a proud and unyielding spirit. Conscious of her infirmity, Lalouette wanted to do things for herself, despising assistance—despising herself.

Her father could not bring himself to look at her. When she was seventeen years old her mother died and her father sent her away with her nurse. "All the money that you need, take," he said, "only do not let me see this abortion." Then, when the first World War came, the count lost all his money and shot himself.

The kind old nurse lost much of her kindness after that, and when an agent named Geefler offered her money if she could persuade the girl to go with him, the nurse, pleading sickness and poverty, had no difficulty in persuading Lalouette that this would be a good thing to do.

So the young lady changed her name. Geefler sold her to Gargamelov, who passed her on to Faragut; and she drew money up and down the world, until Faragut's Circus went toward Mexico, and the *Anna Maria* was wrecked, and she found herself with Tick and Tack and Gargantua the Horror on Porcosito, the Island of Pigs.

Then the prophecy came to pass. She was the Queen of Pig Island. She had three subjects: two dancing dwarfs and the ugliest and strongest man in the word; and she had no arms and no legs; and she was beautiful.

Gargantua was a man whose tenderness was in inverse proportion to his frightful ugliness. As soon as the *Anna Maria* began to sink he went instinctively to the weakest of his friends and offered them his muscles.

To Tick and Tack he said, "Hold on to my shoulders." They were in sight of land. He took Lalouette in his left hand, told the others to hold tight, and jumped overboard, and swam with his legs and his right hand. The ship went down. The Horror swam steadily. He must have covered five miles in the face of a falling high wind.

At last his feet touched ground and he staggered up to a sandy beach as the sun was rising. The two little men were clinging to him still. His left hand, stronger than the iron which it could bend, held Lalouette. The dwarfs dropped off like gorged leeches, and the giant threw himself down and went to sleep—but not before he had made a hollow place in the soft, fine sand and put Lalouette comfortably to rest.

It was then, I believe, that Gargantua fell in love with Lalouette. I have seen it happen myself—in less outrageous circumstances, thank God! The strong makes itself the slave of the weak. And he saved her life. It is the tendency of Man to love that which he has risked his life to save.

Unhappy Gargantua! Poor Horror!

Armless and legless, Lalouette was the Brain. In spite of her disability she was the Queen of Pig Island. She was without hope and devoid of fear; so she could command, since everything was clear in her mind. And she had read many books.

Lalouette said, "Tick and Tack; there must be water here. One of you go to the left. The other goes to the right. Look for the place where things grow greenest—"

"Who d'you think you are, giving orders?" said Tick.

She said, "Oh yes, and another thing; empty your pockets."

Tick had, among other things, a leather-covered loose-leaf notebook. Tack had a remarkably large-bladed knife which he carried, no doubt, to give himself confidence; but he was a fierce little man at heart. They all had money. Gargantua had a fine gold cigarette-lighter, and a few hundred sodden dollars in a sea-soaked pocket—he alone wore no grouch bag. Lalouette had strung about her neck with her grouch bag a gold pencil.

"We'll need all these things," she said.

"Who the hell d'you think you are, giving us orders?" said Tick.

"Be quiet," said Gargantua.

Lalouette continued, "That lighter is of no use as a lighter, because it's full of water. But it has flint and steel; it strikes a spark. Good. Gargantua, leave it to dry."

"Yes'm."

"You two, on your way right and left, had better pick up dry driftwood—the drier the better. We can strike a spark with that lighter and make a fire. Having lit a fire we can keep it burning. It must not ever be allowed to go out. Your knife, Tack, will be useful too. . . . You, Gargantua, will go up the beach. There is a lot of wood here from ships. So there must be iron. Wood from ships has always iron. Iron is always useful. In any case bring wood that has been cut. We will build a little house. You shall built it, Gargantua—and you too, Tick, and you also, Tack. I shall tell you how you must build it."

Tick began to protest. "Who d'you think—"

"Leave the lighter so that it dries in the sun," said Lalouette, "and take care that your knife is dry and clean, Tack."

"Always," said Tack.

Gargantua said, "Here's my lighter; you can have it if you like—it's solid gold. A lady gave me it in France. She said—"

"You can have my notebook if you like," said Tick sullenly. "It's solid leather, that cover. Pull that gadget down and those rings open and the pages come out."

"Please, if you will allow me, I will keep my knife," said Tack.

"You may keep your knife," said Lalouette. "But remember that we may all need it, your knife."

"Naturally, Mademoiselle Lalouette."

"Who does she think—" began Tick.

"Shush!" said Gargantua.

"No offense, Lalouette?" said Tick.

"Go now, please. Go!"

They went. Tick found a spring of fresh water. Tack reported the presence of wild pigs. Gargantua returned with an armful of wreckage; wood spiked with rusty nails; a massive thing like a broken mast in which was embedded an enormous iron pin.

"Light the fire," said Lalouette. "You, Gargantua, make a spear of that long piece of iron. Make it sharp with stones.

Then tie it tight to a stick. So you can kill pigs. You and you, Tick and Tack, go up to the rocks. I have seen birds coming down. Where there are birds there are eggs. You are light, you are dancers. Find eggs. Better still, find birds. When they sit on their eggs they are reluctant to go far away from their nests. Approach calmly and quietly, lie still, and then take them quickly. Do you understand?"

"Beautifully," said Tack.

Tick said nothing.

"Better get that fire going first of all," said Gargantua.

Lalouette said, "True. Boats must pass and they will see the smoke. Good, light the fire."

"If I could find another bit of iron, or something heavy," said Gargantua, "I could do better than this spiky sort of thing, Miss. I dare say I could bang it out to a bit of a blade once I got the fire going good and hot."

"How?" said Lalouette.

"I was 'prentice to a blacksmith, 'm," said Gargantua. "My dad was a smith, before the motorcars came in."

"What? You have skill then, in those great hands of yours?"

"Yes'm. Not much. A bit, but not much."

"Then make your 'bit of a blade,' Gargantua."

"Thank you, 'm."

"Can you make me a comb?"

"Why, I daresay yes. Yes, I should say I *could* make you a bit of a comb, 'm. But nothing fancy," said Gargantua, shutting one eye and calculating. "Something out of a little bit of wood, like."

"Do so, then."

"Yes'm. If Mr. Tack doesn't mind me using his knife."

"Could you also build a house, Gargantua?"

"No 'm, not a house; but I daresay I might put you up a bit of a shed, like. Better be near the drinking water, though. And I shouldn't be surprised if there was all sorts of bits of string along the beach. Where there's sea there's fish. And don't you worry—I'll bring you home a nice pig, only let me get that fire going nice and bright. And as for fish," said Gargantua, plucking a nail out of a plank and making a hook of it between a finger and thumb—"sharpen that up and there you are."

"Clever!" said Tick, with malice.

"But he always was clever," said Tack tonelessly, but with a bitter little smile. "We already know."

Gargantua blinked, while Lalouette said, "Be quiet, please, both of you."

Then Gargantua nodded and growled, "That's right. You be quiet."

Tick and Tack exchanged glances and said nothing until Lalouette cried, "Come! To work!"—when Tick muttered, "Who the hell do they think they are, giving orders?"

"Come on now, you two!" shouted Gargantua.

I believe it was then that the two midgets Tick and Tack began to plot and conspire against Gargantua the Horror, and I am convinced that they too in their dwarfish way were in love with Lalouette.

They followed Lalouette's instructions, and struck sparks out of Gargantua's lighter to kindle powdery flakes of dry driftwood whittled with Tack's big-bladed knife. Tick blew the smolder into flame and the men fed the fire until it blazed red-hot, so that Gargantua, having found a thick slab and a pear-shaped lump of hard rock for his anvil and hammer, beat his iron spike into a good spearhead which he lashed to a long, strong pole. Then they had a crude but effective pike, with which Gargantua killed wild pigs.

Porcosito is not called Pig Island without reason. It used to be overrun with swine, bred from a pedigree boar and some sows that Sir John Page sent to Mexico in 1893, in the *Ponce de Leon*, which was wrecked in a squall. Only the pigs swam ashore from that shipwreck. Porcosito seems to be an unlucky island.

Gargantua hunted ruthlessly. The pigs were apathetic. The boars charged—to meet the spear. The four freaks ate well. Tick and Tack fished and caught birds, gathered eggs and crabs. Lalouette directed everything and at night, by the fire, told them stories and sang to them, recited all the poetry she could remember, and dug out of her memory all she had ever read of philosophy.

I believe that they were happy then; but it makes an odd picture: the truncated beauty, the stunted dancers and the ugliest man on earth, grouped about a flickering fire while the songs of Schubert echo from the rocks and the sea says *hush . . . hush . . .* on the beach. I can see the sharp, keen faces of the midgets; and the craggy forehead of the giant wrinkled in anguish as he tries to understand the inner significance of great thoughts expressed in noble words. She told them stories, too, of the heroes of ancient Greece and Rome—of Regulus, who went back to Carthage to die; of the glorious dead at Thermopylae, and of the wise and cunning Ulysses, the subtlest of the Greeks, who strove with gods and came home triumphant at last. She told them of the triumph of Ulysses over Circe, the sorceress who turned men into beasts; and how he escaped with his crew from the cave of the one-eyed giant Cyclops. He was colossal; the men were small. Ulysses drilled his sailors to move like one man and, with a sharpened stick, blinded the giant and escaped.

She let them comb her hair. The French dwarf Tack was skillful at this, and amusing in conversational accompaniment to the crackling of the hair and the fire. Tick hated his partner for this. Yet the gigantic hands of Gargantua were lighter on her head than the hands of Tick or Tack—almost certainly because the little men wanted to prove that they were strong, and the giant wanted to demonstrate that he was gentle.

It was Gargantua who combed Lalouette's beautiful bright hair, evening after evening, while Tick and Tack sat exchanging looks. No words; only looks.

Sometimes the little men went hunting with Gargantua. Alone, neither Tick nor Tack could handle the heavy spear. But it must be remembered that they were a dancing team, trained to move together in perfect accord. So, while Tick directed the forepart of the shaft, Tack worked close behind him, and they put their combined, perfectly synchronized strength and agility into a dangerous leap-and-lunge. Once they killed a fat boar. This must have made them confident of their power to kill.

This is not all guesswork. I have ground for my assumption, in what Lalouette wrote in Tick's loose-leaf notebook, holding the gold pencil in her teeth and guiding it with her lips, before she bit the paper into a ball and pushed it with her tongue into her grouch bag.

It takes courage and determination to kill a wild boar with a spear. A boar is fearless, powerful, unbelievably ferocious, and armored with hard hide and thick muscle. He is wickedly obstinate—a slashing fury, a ripping terror—two sickles on a battering-ram, animated by a will to kill, uninhibited by fear of death.

Having killed a boar, Tick and Tack, in their pride, resolved to kill Gargantua.

Lalouette says that she, unwittingly, gave them the idea, when she told them the story of Ulysses and Cyclops.

But the foolish giant called Gargantua the Horror, billed as the strongest and ugliest man on earth, must have been easy to kill. He worked all day. When Lalouette's hair was combed and her singing ceased, he went away modestly to sleep in the bushes. One night, after he had retired, Tick and Tack followed him. Gargantua always carried the spear. Lalouette listened drowsily for the comforting rumble of Gargantua's snoring a few yards away; she loved him, in a sisterly way.

. . . *Ha-khaaa . . . kha-ha . . . khaaaa-huk . . . khaaaa . . .*

As she listened, smiling, the snoring stopped with a gasp. Then Tick and Tack came back carrying the spear, and in the firelight Laloutte could see that the blade of the spear was no longer clean. The redness of it was not a reflected redness.

Thus she knew what the little men had done to Gargantua. She would have wept if she could; but there was no hand to wipe away her tears, and she was a proud woman. So she forced herself to pretend to be asleep.

Later she wrote: *I knew that this was the end. I was sorry. In this place I have felt strangely calm and free, happier than I have ever been since my dear mother used to hold me in her arms and tell me all the stories I told here; stories of gods and heroes and pygmies and giants, and of men with wings . . .*

But that night, looking through the lashes of her half-closed eyes, she saw Tick untying the blade of the spear. He worked for an hour before he got it loose, and then he had a sort of dirk, more than a foot long, which he concealed in a trouser-leg. Tack, she thought, had been watching him also; for as soon as Tick closed his eyes and began to breathe evenly, he took out the knife which he had never allowed them to take away from him, and stabbed his partner through the heart.

He carried the body out of the range of her vision, and left it where he let it fall—Lalouette never knew where.

Next morning Tack said to her, "At last we are alone. You are my Queen."

"The fire?" she said, calmly.

"Ah yes. The fire. I will put wood on the fire, and then perhaps we may be alone after all this time."

Tack went away and Lalouette waited. He did not return. The disposition of his bones, and the scars on them, indicate that he was killed by a boar. There was no more driftwood nearby. Tack went into the trees to pick up whatever he might find. As I visualize it, he stooped to gather sticks, and looked up into the furious and bloody eyes of a great angry boar gathering itself for a charge. This must be so; there is no other way of accounting for the scattering of his shattered bones. Hence, the last thing Tack saw must have been the bristly head of a pig, a pair of curled tusks, and two little red eyes. . . .

The last words in what may be described as Lalouette's Journal are as follows:

A wind is blowing. The fire is dying. God grant that my end may be soon.

This is the history of the Queen of Pig Island, and of the bones Captain Oxford found.

PROPHET WITHOUT HONOR

Time is a liar and a tease. Time is a confidence trickster. Time sells you that which is not, and which never has been. The Devil makes capital by selling Retrospect in three dimensions to fools like Faust who, at the cost of their immortal souls, want to capture their "youth." How often have we heard the voice of ulcerated misery, wise with the wisdom of a quarter of a century of interoffice knife-play, groaning in one of those discreetly dim bars off Madison Avenue: *If only I could have my time over again!* . . . Or in Michael's Pub off Fifth Avenue, or the Absinthe House on the West Side, about 12:45 any afternoon, watched it feeling the tatty fur on its tongue with its loose-fitting false teeth, and talking out of the corner of its mouth furthest away from you (for fear of offending you with bad breath) of what might have been perhaps, would be whether, and should have been if . . .

Si la jeunesse savait! Si la vieillesse pouvait!—so yearns the catchword, meaning: "If youth had the experience of old age; and old age the vigor of youth!" These French epigrams go down smoothly, but stick in the discriminating craw; could anything be more repulsive than a teen-ager, in all his frenetic vigor, with the outlook, the libido, and the untickled appetites of a decadent old playboy? . . . The most incorrigible Time-Over-Againers are generally to be found in the self-huckstering professions—I mean advertising men, real estate speculators, moving picture men, journalists, and the like—people who are incredibly wise long after the event. These young-old-timers must necessarily be one jump behind competition; they are living on borrowed time.

Some of the very worst offenders in this respect are the elderly, brilliant desk-men, features men, and editorial writers in newspaper row. They earn good money and are much looked up to; newspaper cubs are honored by their attention and, figuratively speaking, hang on their leaden or purple lips. More often than not they are generous with their money, and with their advice; and if there is one kind of person they like better than the worldly wise one whom they knew "when," it is the eager youngster with ideals to denigrate. Their cynicism is sad, kindly, even paternal . . . but it is, nonetheless, the voice of weariness and disillusionment. Toward the end of the evening, when they are expected at home, where their friends are not welcome, they generally say, with a lingering, nostalgic, affectionate handshake, "Ah, my boy, if I were *your* age!" And when they leave you have a feeling of something lost, or rather mislaid; in some pyramidal shadow in one of the corners of the pub they have left something of themselves behind, something ragged with disuse. . . .

When I was in Fleet Street—which is, in London, what newspaper row once was in New York—the night editor of *The Daily Special* was such a man. His name was Bohemund Raymond, and his incapacity for hard liquor had made him notorious from Blackfriars to Temple Bar. (I say "incapacity," on the assumption that a capacious man can drink a lot without getting drunk.) I believe that his appearance of drunkenness was exaggerated by a peculiar habit of speech: he spoke with a Devon drawl, and had, moreover, that inability to pronounce two successive consonants which is supposed to be characteristic of the Arabs. Take, say, the word *strong*: Bohemund Raymond would pronounce it something like "issitirong." Once, in the Punch Tavern, some old soldier, half-demented with malaria, who had been trying to sell an article about elephants' tusks during the silly season, had the nerve to say, in Bohemund Raymond's hearing, "No, I mean to say, blast it! Was in Palestine with Allenby, blast it! I talk Wog. That man talks with a *chi-chi*, like a confounded Wog. No, really, I mean to say, after all, what?" Whereupon Bohemund Raymond looked at the man steadily for a long time, and said, in his peculiarly resonant voice, "By 'Wog' I take it this derelict means 'Arab.' Why, of course! By God, my fathers took Antioch when this fellow's people were herding swine! Damn it," shouted Bohemund Raymond, pointing to one of the arteries in his throat, "in this vein flows the blood of Bohemund, of Richard Lion-Heart, of Godfrey de Bouillon! My ancestress was a Saracen princess. Damn your eyes, my own mother was named after her—Asia Raymond, short for Ayesha! . . . 'Wog!' "

The old soldier, fatuous with bottled beer, said, "No, but really, I mean to say, after all—what I mean, all those fathers, eh, and only one mother, what?" Then Bohemund Raymond said: "I'll 'Wog' you,"—and so he did, with a pewter pot. And he saw to it that the article about elephants' tusks was rejected the following day; threatened, indeed, to resign if it was accepted. . . . It was not that Bohemund Raymond was mean, or vindictive; in general, he was very generous and, in a quarrel, magnanimous. Only he could not bear to be touched in his ticklish spot: his ancestry.

As everybody knows, Phoenician blood ran strong in the west of England, where his family came from, so that to this day you may see hawk-faced, black-avised, strangely clannish, subtle, proud and quarrelsome alien-looking men and women around Marazion. But Bohemund Raymond disclaimed descent from these Vikings of the Levant. No; he insisted that he was a lineal descendant of a great crusader and the Princess Ayesha who, he emphasized, was divinely inspired, a prophetess, something like Cassandra of Troy, only more so. He would recount with extraordinary vividness the circumstances of her prediction about the Battle of the Spear: It seems that Ayesha, after she was carried off, baptized out of hand, and married to his ancestor, had a revelation in a dream of a buried spearhead which, said Ayesha, was a holy relic; it had been used by a Roman soldier at the foot of the Cross, so that whoever followed it must be certain of victory. The spearhead was dug up, the crusaders followed it as a banner, and won a wonderful fight. Telling of this, with a wild, faraway look in his dark-pouched black eyes, Bohemund would say, "And I, too, my friends, shall perish by the ancient bronze spear in the right hand of my ancient hereditary enemy!"

When he had drink taken—and when had he not?—Bohemund Raymond frequently made such cryptic oracular prophecies. We happened to remember this one, when he died of blood poisoning in the summer of 1939, having run a rusty brass paper fastener into his left thumb. He had drunk himself out of half a dozen important jobs in Fleet Street—gulped himself down; as I may say, swallowed himself—so that at the time of his death he was fiction editor of *The Evening Special*, a creature whom we fiction writers liked to whisper of as one of the lowest forms of life.

The news of his death was received as the news of such deaths is generally received in the newspaper rows of all the cities in the world. There were the maudlin ones who, having made their reputations in other lines of the business, and seeing in this minor tragedy the handwriting on their own walls growled, "We won't see *his* like again," and went to the Press Club in search of more mourners of their generation. There were cubs, gnashing their milk-teeth among the umbles, the scattered guts of the big kills, who, hoping one day to pull down their own bull, watched for a forward movement in the pack. Some gloated: The elephant-tusk man maintained that it was his story that had caused the death of Bohemund Raymond; he said that it was still going the rounds, pinned together by the same paper fastener, which was covered with verdigris (his pension was not due until next Tuesday and, meanwhile, although he hated to accept a drink without being able to return it . . . et cetera . . .). An old advertising man, who had entertainment-expensed himself into the gutter of the small-ad peddlers, said that Bohemund Raymond had survived that long by blackmailing Lord Lovejoy, the baron who owned *The Daily Special*, *The Evening Special*, and *The Sunday Special*; trust Bohemund to know where the body was buried, he said, with a beery wink, nodding like a porcelain chinaman . . . until one of the old guard, "Swindle-sheet" Morris, gasping over half an inch of cigarette—mysteriously, he never had more or less than half an inch of cigarette—told him to be damned for a dirty little advertising man.

Bohemund Raymond would never soil his hands on such, said "Swindle-sheet" Morris, "but I don't mind if I do, you little mess, you! Bohemund was my friend, and I say so to the whole bleeding pub-load of you. You are not fit to drink the water he washed his socks in, and if any of you want to deny it, come on! Single-handed, or mob-handed, come on! . . . Will you stand by, Gerald?"

I said, "Oh, sure, Morris."

Then, with emotion, "Swindle-sheet" Morris said, "We knew him in good times and bad, old Bohemund—didn't we, Gerald? We were cubs under Bohemund; weren't we, Gerald? Why, when the old *World-Globe* went bust and was bought by Lovejoy in 1929, who predicted it? Bohemund Raymond! Why, you little layabouts, I see him as plain as I see you here—plainer—saying: 'Morris, the world is coming to an end, and the very globe will change.' And that, mind you, was in 1917. . . . Bohemund was like a mother and father to me: he tore up every word I wrote, he treated me like a dog, he bashed me into shape, he made me what I am. Didn't he, Gerald?"

Since I could not very well say that I did not remember, and that, in any case, while "Swindle-sheet" Morris was what he was, I did not much care for his shape, I could only say, "You've got something there, Morris."

At this, Jack Cantwhistle, the old crime reporter, a kindly, sensitive man under the scar-tissue, said: "Yes, Bohemund was the ablest man in the Street. God knows what he might have got to be if it wasn't for his 'ifs and ans.' Poor old Bohemund always had to *foresee*—no part of a newspaperman's job, foreseeing; very dangerous practice. We're all entitled to a bit of guesswork; but you keep your guesses to yourself. I'm not saying a word against my old friend Bohemund, Morris, and I won't hear a word said against him—only, when he had one of his funny turns, especially after he'd been on a blind, he had to get prophetic. Made himself a laughing-stock, in fact."

"Swindle-sheet" Morris said, "Laugh if you like, Jack—his prophecies always came true, almost. When he first took me on, I worshiped the ground he trod on. But he said to me, 'Get on the job. Keep your thanks. You will live to make a hissing and a mockery of me!' And Lord forgive me, so I did. . . . And as for my old friend Bohemund's having a glass of beer once in a while between meals; why, he *had* to, because he took things so much to heart. He got away from the world that way, and clarified his intellect."

The decayed advertising man sniggered. "Bohemund clarified his intellect all right, that time Lord Lovejoy sent him to Scotland for six months! Remember? The time he started seeing snakes and mermaids and midgets and things in the office?"

"Swindle-sheet" Morris shouted: "Why, you lavatory! Bohemund's intellect was never clearer than when he saw those snakes, et cetera. They said it was d.t.'s, but it wasn't. I know, because I was his assistant, at the time, damn it all! . . ." Then he went on to say that, at that time, in the spring of 1930, Bohemund's wife ran away from him. To her, as to everyone else, he had prophesied "You shall make a hissing and a mockery of me." And so she did. He went on working, however, with deadly efficiency but like a man in a dream, souping himself up for the superhuman efforts of each new night with whisky—as a robber soups up an old stolen car for the few minutes of a mad dash between the smashing of the jeweler's window and the hideout. So Bohemund Raymond blasted and rattled from sunset to sunrise, leaving behind him a trail of startled faces, shattered glass and shrill whistles.

Now those who say that Lord Lovejoy tolerated Bohemund Raymond because that phenomenal newspaperman "had something on him" do the memory of the Press Baron an injustice. Everyone had something on Lord Lovejoy; those who hadn't, invented something to have on him, and much he cared! Lord Lovejoy was a ruthless man, an unscrupulous man, a pig-headed and, at times, brutal man; but he was neither a coward nor a fool. He liked you or he didn't, often for the wrong reasons; but he was as staunch a friend as he was implacable an enemy. One evening—you could never predict the movements of Lord Lovejoy—returning from Canada where he had just bought five hundred square miles of virgin forest to shred up and pulp for his newspapers, he looked in at the office, dressed in a mackinaw. The night doorman, who was drunk and new to the job, asked him who the devil he thought he was. "I am Lord Lovejoy," said the little potentate. "Oh yes? And I am Bombardier Billy Wells," said the doorman, using the name of the man who was at that time heavyweight boxing champion of England. . . . Lord Lovejoy then said, "And how do you like *The Daily Special*?" The doorman said, "Och, I wouldn't use it to wrap tripe-and-chips in. Indade, I wouldn't carry the damned rag away with me atall, atall, only my little bhoy likes to color in the fashion section, bless his heart, wid his little box o' paints."

At this point, Lord Lovejoy's secretary arrived, breathless, and took his master upstairs to the office with the onyx desk. There, Lord Lovejoy said, "That man Bombardier Billy Wells— take him off the door. Start a new children's section; make him editor; get circulation. What we need is an Empire-wide printing competition for children under fourteen—five thousand pounds in prizes and scholarships. . . . You were three minutes late; you're fired. . . . Where's Bohemund Raymond? Never mind, I'll go myself. . . ." So Lord Lovejoy walked into the news room, and there was Bohemund Raymond drinking a colorless liquid that smelled of juniper berries out of a teacup. The night's work was nearly over. Poor Raymond's right hand was bleeding—he had impaled it on the spike, that stake which is driven through the heart of rejected copy. Lord Lovejoy said to him, "Hello, Raymond! See anything new?" Then Bohemund replied, in his double-clipped sonorous voice, "Serpents! Maddened beasts! Yes, I see a Mermaid, and a tiger—and a giraffe looking in the window. Between his legs run little wizened dwarfs in—"

"You've been on the booze, Bohemund, old man," said Lord Lovejoy, "and you'd better lay off. Come on, after all, I bar seeing snakes in office hours. Take three months' holiday with pay, and go to my place in Scotland. One more peep out of you, and I'll fire you." Then he called his secretary and said, "Oh, Spray—you were three minutes late tonight; losing grip; need vacation. So does Bohemund Raymond; pack up and go to Loch Lovejoy with him at once; but if I hear only one drop—one drop, mind!—of liquor has passed his lips in the next twelve weeks, as from this moment, you are fired this time once and for all. Get cracking!" After a few more serious words with Bohemund Raymond, the Press Baron concluded: ". . . I have your solemn word of honor then—no liquor for three months. Otherwise you're through. Meet Spray, and scram; anything extraordinary happens, let me know. 'Bye now."

So Bohemund Raymond left for Scotland with the teetotal secretary, Spray. They had not been gone ten hours when one of Lord Lovejoy's private phones rang, by one of his bedsides, and the voice of Bohemund Raymond, shaky but calm, said, "You said to tell you if anything extraordinary happens. Raymond calling from Dogworthy Junction. Listen, the mermaid is dying on the platform. One of the seven dwarfs has broken his leg, and his tiny wife is tying up his wounds with her spangled tights. Hold on! There is a tiger loose in the streets, and a rat with orange-colored teeth, five feet long, chewing tobacco—and the giraffe, poor beast, cut his neck on the glass of my window—" Abruptly, Lord Lovejoy rang off, got through to the office and said, "Fire Raymond and Spray." Next morning, however, there was a report of the affair in all the other papers: Bohemund Raymond's train had collided with a circus train, and for a few hours many of the side-show exhibits were loose around Dogworthy Junction.

The Mermaid, an unhappy Manatee cow that was depicted on the posters as a voluptuous blonde with a fish's tail, combing her hair at a hand-glass and singing melodiously, but that looked in fact like a sea-elephant with breasts, fell out of her tank of salt water and bellowed her last at the station-master's feet. The Biggest Rat in the World—a capybara, or water-pig— ran away on its long legs and settled down in a nearby kitchen garden, the owner of which, a maiden lady who was afraid of mice, went out of her mind. One of a team of midget acrobats did, indeed, break his leg—*The Daily Flash* ran a big picture of his wife, thirty inches high, applying first aid. A spavined giraffe sustained injuries from broken glass, and a tiger, too old and broken-spirited to care, had to be carried back to its cage by six volunteers, led by the local policeman who directed operations with a pitchfork. Thus, Lord Lovejoy sent a Memo: *Unfire Raymond and Spray*; and Bohemund Raymond was back in the office within a week, drunker than ever. . . .

. . . Although everyone in Fleet Street had been laughing over that story for years, now Morris found no pleasure in it; there was grief in his heart. He said to me, "Let's get out of here, Gerald, and I'll tell you how *I* made a hissing and a mockery of poor old Bohemund Raymond. God knows, it was all in fun. I might say, in fact, that the joke I played on him had a salubrious effect, because he didn't touch drink in any form afterward until just before he died. But he found out about the trick I played on him, and I don't think he ever forgave me for it . . . but confidentially, between us, you know, he *did* ask for it. . . . Walk back to my place and I'll tell you. . . ."

"Swindle-sheet" Morris had a three-room flat over a secondhand furniture shop in Red Lion Street. He found some bottled beer, two packets of potato-crisps and a jar of pickled red cabbage, and made room for them on the sitting-room table by pushing aside a typewriter, a hat and a little box of laundry ready for the wash. "It's a little stuffy," he said, "but I don't like to open the window in case the papers get blown away." He sniffed, and added: "Yes, I burned some kippers the day before yesterday; and all that junk, those sofas and mattresses downstairs, *do* have a bit of a pong. Miracle how the old crook finds a market for 'em. . . . See that typewriter? That's *the* typewriter—"

It was a big, old-fashioned desk model, badly battered, such as you may see in any newspaper office; a rakish, promiscuous, disreputable old typewriter, it had submitted to hard usage by a thousand pairs of heavy hands and adjusted itself to none. On the front of the frame, heavily stenciled, was the inscription: PROPERTY OF LOVEJOY PRESS—NOT TO BE TAKEN AWAY!

"His typewriter, Bohemund's typewriter," said "Swindle-sheet" Morris. "He took a fancy to it and wouldn't let anybody else use it—he said it *knew* him; said it practically typed of its own accord. So I pinched it for a keepsake, after he died. Of course, I daresay you know Bohemund Raymond really was a marvelous touch-typist, faster and more accurate than any girl in the office, and the funny thing is the tighter he got, the faster he got. Well, you remember Bohemund's bragging about that so-called Saracen priestess and that crusader; and, sometimes, boasting about what he called his 'Gift of Prophecy,' and, then again, his 'Infallible Accuracy' on this typewriter. He called it 'Rataplan'—which, according to his cock-and-bull story, was the name of an old war horse that belonged to this ancestor of his: it seems this here horse was stone-blind in both eyes, and still the best charger in the crusades because it couldn't see danger. Well, you know Bohemund and I were always the best of friends; but there comes a time when even your best friend can get on your nerves a bit—especially in a year like 1938, when every lousy office boy went around prophesying like Isaiah, and doubting whether they had done wisely putting Chamberlain in power.

"That was the time when everybody knew all about everything. You remember: Hitler, Goering and Co. were drug fiends and drunkards and lunatics; and there weren't any real generals in the German Army because Hitler had shot them all and put cocaine addicts and perverts in their places; and how the German Army was mostly propaganda—Goebbels had one crack company of infantry march past a camera and ran the same reel six times over. Even my charwoman used to wake me up in the morning with the impregnability of the Maginot Line and gallant little Belgium.... Of course old Bohemund Raymond was a thousand times worse than anybody else, especially since old Lovejoy had put him onto writing that famous series of editorials that always ended: *What Are You Going To Do About It?*—like Cato's: *Carthage Must Be Destroyed!* He was having the time of his life, old Bohemund, prophesying to his heart's content. We had to cut the juiciest bits; but even what was left took a gloomy, frightening turn. Lord Lovejoy was able to say, 'I told you so' later on; but those editorials didn't make us very popular at the time.

"And all the while Bohemund was drinking like a drain. He went on steadily till three o'clock in the Pig's Head; knocked off for a quick sandwich, and was at it again in the Press Club until about an hour before his deadline. He'd just about manage to get to the office and flop into his chair. Then it was marvelous to watch him: he got steady as a rock—couldn't see an inch in front of him, he was so pickled, but he didn't have to; he'd snap in a sheet of copy paper and rattle off a thousand words of perfect prose, touch-typing like a conjurer, and staring into space with those big shiny eyes so as to give you the creeps. It would be all over in forty-five minutes. The boy would pick up the copy and Bohemund would fall into a taxi and go home. Well, one day Lord Lovejoy sent him to France to look at the Maginot Line. He locked up his old typewriter Rataplan as usual and gave me the key of the cupboard to hold; and when he was gone, I got this wicked idea of mine. . . .

"I went to a typewriter mechanic, a pal of mine, and I said to him, 'Alf, there's a little job I want you to do for me, just for a lark. Take all the letters off the type-bars on this machine, and put them back all jumbled up. Leave the keys as they are, only mix me up all the letters; so that, for instance, if somebody hits an *A*, he'll get a question-mark, and so forth. Only you've got to be ready to put that type back exactly as it was before, overnight, at an hour's notice. There's a fiver in it for you,' I said. And so he did. I locked old Rataplan back in her cupboard and waited. Couple of days later Bohemund turns up again in the Pig's Head, full to the gills with armagnac, and went straight onto gin. He took his key, and when we asked him, 'What news, Bohemund? What do you know?' he simply turned round and said, 'You wait and see!'—nothing more. But his eyes were full of something more dangerous than brandy; I thought: *Either he's drunk himself off his rocker at last or he's in a bad fever.*

"Now I had to go out of town for the afternoon. I kept thinking about the trick I'd played, and at last I phoned the Press

Club to warn him to use some other machine. But he'd left already, having told a few fellows that he was going to astound the world with the greatest prophecy of all time. I buzzed the office: Bohemund had staggered in, got out Rataplan, touch-typed his piece as usual and reeled out, shouting, 'It is achieved! I've done it!' As soon as I got back to town late that night, I went straight to the office, where there was some little excitement about Bohemund's copy. . . . When the Editor saw the piece he yelled blue murder for Bohemund, but he was nowhere to be found. It appears that instead of going home he'd gone to the Turkish bath in Jermyn Street, where they had to call the police; seems he wrapped himself in towels and made a veil of a check-loincloth, and stood in the hot room screaming gibberish. When they hauled him out, finally, he said he was the Princess Ayesha, prophesying. They recognized him at the station and didn't charge him, so he went and slept it off. Meantime I got Alf to fix up the machine again, having, of course, had a duplicate key made for the cupboard; and put it back as Bohemund left it.

"First thing in the morning Lord Lovejoy phoned him and told him to come around to the office, immediately if not sooner; which he did. Now what was said at that interview I never quite knew, but knowing old Lovejoy I can pretty well guess. So I didn't feel easy in my mind when I went to the Pig's Head for a pie at noon; but when Bohemund came in I was absolutely appalled by his face—it was always pale in a creamy kind of way; now it was like curds and whey. The barmaid reached automatically for the gin, but Bohemund said, 'A ginger-ale, if you please, Miss Broom.' She nearly dropped the bottle, she was so surprised. He said to me, 'Morris, I'm on the wagon—I'm on the wagon for life. Look at this.' And he fished out of his pocket some copy paper, crumpled into a ball. 'Lovejoy chucked it in my face,' he said. 'He threatened to fire me, as usual, but when I saw this stuff, for the first time in my life I could only apologize. I said something must have gone wrong with my typewriter. Then Lovejoy asked me, well, what *was* this famous leader I had been shouting about? *And for the life of me I couldn't remember a word of it!* I went back to look at old Rataplan. Morris—there is nothing wrong with my typewriter! I must have gone out of my mind. Chuck this stuff away, Morris, and promise me you'll never breathe a word of this to a soul.'

"I promised, and I kept my word. But Alf squealed in the end and, as Bohemund had prophesied, I was responsible for making a bigger hissing and mockery of him than anyone else in the Street. But before he found out, he didn't touch a drink for close on a year; so perhaps he was the better for it, after all."

"Swindle-sheet" Morris opened a drawer and rummaged in a litter of souvenirs—racing cards, autographed menus, and what not—and took out some crumpled yellow flimsy copy paper. He said, "I didn't chuck it away; I kept it. I'm funny about mementos. Can you imagine old Lovejoy's face when he saw this?"

I took the copy and read:

Waf iakh er aaumqa Ibala ssad tunsabal mash naqatal ruma niyaa andzu hooralhi lalalga deed.

O ulanya squtay uhuma. Hak azac at taraal qadar.

Way a tazauag alhila lwal sa leebta khtb urgad dubzee al alf rigl waya temzali kfeea amda mual ginse eal ass faree.

Way a tazauag assal eebalkhu ttafmaa ssal eebalma akcof feel nari waldami khennayal tahermua lkhamlual assad takhtal qadeebwa ifas wassal eebal maksoor.

Way a ssaadual assa dubaadi zali kmaalni srwatu alaq alduf daamin aqda miha.

Waf eehazi hialsa na alsa natalkham soonmin kharbal alfazya assoo duassala amqem mamana alatwar tafa at fau qaalkhar abiwa alaanqa adialar dalmah rooka.

"I can just imagine," I said. "Mind if I take a copy?"

"If you like, Gerald," "Swindle-sheet" Morris said gloomily. "Only if you write the yarn and sell it to a magazine, you might remember to give me a twenty-five per cent cut, old man?"

I might never have written it if my old friend, Dr. Marengo, had not come to my house to wish me bon voyage when I was leaving for America in April, 1955. Dr. Marengo is best known, of course, as Kem, the cartoonist; but he is also famous as a political scientist, an expert on international law and a linguist: he speaks and writes seventeen European and Oriental languages with perfect fluency and accuracy. While we chatted as old friends will, I was turning over an old box-file full of unconsidered scraps of paper. And there, among hieroglyphic notes which had lost their meaning and newspaper clippings the significance of which I had forgotten, I found my copy of Bohemund Raymond's leader.

I handed it to Kem and said, "You're good at cryptograms. What do you make of this one?" He took the paper, put in his monocle and stopped eating salted peanuts for several minutes while he concentrated on the words before him.

Then he said, "But my dear Gerald, this is not a cryptogram at all. It is, actually, pure Arabic written phonetically, as far as that is possible, in Roman letters—only some of the words are broken up and others are run together. One needs only to read it aloud, and it becomes quite clear."

"Arabic?" I said. "Did I hear you say *Arabic*?"

"Certainly—

Wafi ákher aa 'uam qalf al ássad túnsab al mashnaqat' al rumaniya aand zuhoor al hilál gadeed.
Oulan yasqut ayuhuma. Hákaza sáttara alqádar . . .

. . . means, in English:

In the last year of the heart of the lion, the Roman gallows must stand against new moon.
Neither may fall. So it is written . . .

... That is the accurate pronunciation, and a fair translation, of the first paragraph, for example. Shall I—"

"Roman gallows?" I cried. "That's the cross! New moon—Mohammedan crescent! Last year of the heart of the lion—the crusade, in which Richard the Lion-Hearted died!"

"Exactly, Gerald, in 1199," said Kem. "And what do you make of the second paragraph? . . .

Wayatazduag' alhilál wal' saleeb takht búrg ad'dúb zee al alf rigl, wa yátem' zalik fee aam dámu al ginsee al assfáree . . .

. . . This says, in English:

Cross and crescent moon shall be married under the symbol of the bear with 1,000 legs. This is in the year of the blood of the yellow men . . ."

I said, "Why, Kem, obviously this refers to the U.S.S.R.! The bear with a thousand legs is Russia—cross and crescent moon is meant to be hammer and sickle! Go on!"

Kem said, "Freely translated, the third paragraph says—

Cross and crook shall wed crooked cross in fire and blood when lion is devoured by lamb under rod and axe and broken cross . . ."

I shouted, "The Russo-German Pact! Hammer and sickle shall wed swastika when lion (that's Britain) is devoured by lamb (Hitler's astronomical sign was the Lamb) under Mussolini's fasces and the Nazi swastika!"

Kem said, "The next paragraph is rather interesting—

Wayassá 'adu al ássadu ba'adi zálik maal 'nisr, watu'-alaq dufda'a min aqdámiha . . .

It means:—

"Then the eagle shall rejoice with the lion, and the frog shall be hung by the feet . . .

Surely, Gerald, the Eagle is the United States. That bit must refer to the victory of the Allies and the death of Mussolini, 'the Bull-Frog of the Pontine Marshes.' They did hang him up by the feet, you know."

"Go on! Go on!" I pleaded.

Kem went on: "The last piece is the most interesting of all, really . . .

Wáfee házihi alsána, alsánat' al khamsoon min kharb al alfaz, yassoodu assaláam qemmáman aalat wa 'rtafáat fáuqa alkhárabi waala anqáadi al ard almahrooka . . .

This says, in effect:—

In this year, the 50th year of the war of words, peace shall come in high places above burned earth . . ."

I said, "The fiftieth year of the war of words—that might mean the cold war will last half a century, until, say, 1995. But the next bit about the burned earth; is that H-bombs, or cobalt bombs, or something even worse?"

Kem said, with a shrug, "Where did you get this remarkable document, Gerald?" I told him, then, "Swindle-sheet" Morris's account of the trick he had played on Bohemund Raymond. Kem laughed and said, "Yes, poor Morris loved a joke. If you don't mind my asking—does it occur to you that he might, perhaps, have been playing a trick on you, Gerald?"

"What, in Arabic?" I said. "That would have been too subtle for 'Swindle-sheet' Morris. Besides, remember, this was before the war, back in 1939."

"Of course," said Kem, "I must take in consideration the fact that you, also, are a bit of a joker, and might be playing a trick on me."

"I give you my word of honor I am not!"

"Well, really," said Kem, "all I can say is that it's very strange. . . ." He passed me a piece of paper upon which he had been making notes. "Here is what you gave me translated back. It *is*, unquestionably, pure Arabic. I suggest we regard this as a Fleet Street hoax, Gerald; it will be healthier that way."

And so let it be regarded.

. . . But I wish I knew exactly what Bohemund Raymond, or whatever spirit it was that possessed him, meant exactly by those last two lines. . . . We must wait until 1995, and see. . . .

THE BEGGARS' STONE

The monotony of the plain becomes so heartbreaking that you would thank God for the sight of a withered tree. The land lies flat. The road forks and runs away into the unknown distance. Look east, look west; there is nobody, nothing but dust and grass and a dry, melancholy wind which twists the clouds into tortured shapes. The plain is mournful and legend-haunted.

Dig in it and you may find strange things: skulls scored with scars, bits of metal, defaced coins, weapons which at a touch fall to green powder. It swallows men like a sea. The Tartars passed this way, with the flat-faced riffraff of the Bad Lands. "Where my horses' hoofs have passed no grass grows." But grass has grown; the grass always wins in the end, and it covers everything, humbly bending before the wind, but savagely clutching the earth with its roots—bitter, gluttonous Puszta grass that devours the soil.

I say the road forks and is terribly lonely. But a few paces away from the point at which it divides there stands a stone, incalculably ancient, roughhewn into a rectangular shape, burying itself by its own weight . . . "digging its own grave," as they say in these parts.

It used to lie flat. Now it stands erect. In the place where it used to lie there is a deep hole. Grass has begun to encroach on the stone itself. The hard, pale surface sprouts sparse tufts like an old man's chin. These tufts somehow make the stone look older. By moonlight they give it an appearance of something grotesquely like life.

Three sides of the stone are marked with inscriptions. Bend sideways and you may read initials, names and broken phrases in all the languages of the earth: *J. H.*; *M. B. Hunyadi*; several crosses; "GOD WILL PUNISH THEM," in ancient Slavonic.

In one corner somebody has laboriously hacked out a heart and an arrow. Roman, Greek, Russian, Tartar, Georgian—all alphabets may be found there. There is even the name of one *FA'OUZI*, beautifully carved in curling Arabic. To whom did these names and symbols belong? Only God knows.

The time will come when even these desolate marks will have been rubbed away by the rain and the dust, and then there will be nothing but the tired old stone, imperceptibly disintegrating atom by atom in the loneliness of the plain at the fork of the dreary road.

Why was the stone dropped there? For centuries nobody knew. Tramps used it as a seat, a bed, a kitchen and a meeting place. The friction of their bodies alone had worn little hollows in it. Their weight had helped to press it down. Their names were cut into it. They had nothing but names to leave. Some of them, no doubt, were so poor that they had no names. Men and women who lived and died up and down the interminable roads of Europe; people beyond society; lost souls; the forgotten of God; men without hope; eaters of garbage; beggars for charity; people who lived on their sores and deformities; bear trainers, lone bandits, wandering musicians and contortionists—they all rested on that stone, left their marks if they had marks to leave, and went their ways to their unknown graves.

The plainsmen call it The Beggars' Stone, to this day.

One evening in 1906, two men met at the stone. The first had only one leg. He was a short, squat fellow, wrapped in rubbish, crowned with a cowman's round hat which pressed his ears down, and bearded until he resembled a gray mildewed vegetable rather than a man. The other had an air of crime and misery. Life had crushed him dry and flat, like a grape in a press. His face was a Rosetta Stone of bygone violence—it bore the cuneiform scars of a hatchet, the hieroglyphics of a knife, and the queer marks of broken glass. People had tried to kill that man. He was beyond hope and fear.

"Good evening," he said.

"Good evening."

"Cold."

"Bitter," said the one-legged man, nursing his stump.

"Come far?"

"Far enough. And you?"

"Far enough. Where are you heading for?"

"Buda, maybe. You?"

"Maybe Buda. What's your name? They call me Bicskas."

"Probka." The one-legged man sighed. "Well, the stone still lies here. Many's the night I've slept here."

"Me too. See that dent? It fits my head. It might have been made for me."

"Nice soft stone," said Bicskas, grinning. "It's kind of them to let us have even this much. Ha! A stone. I see you pick the south side. You're no fool. You know the ropes. Good. Have you got any food?"

"I've got some bread," said Probka.

"I've got some bacon," said Bicskas.

"I've got some wine," Probka pulled out a bottle.

"We can have a banquet," muttered Bicskas, grinning again. "Look at this." He displayed the stumps of five cigars.

"Things were not always like this, Bicskas, my brother-in-law."

"You're right. Bacon, bread, wine, cigars. What more could you want? Geese?"

"What I mean to say is, I wasn't always poor like this."

"Who cares?" said Bicskas. "However poor you are there's always a consolation. Somewhere there's someone poorer. You have always got something somebody else wants. I've seen a man knifed in the back in Medvegy's Cellar for a boot—one old boot with a hole in the sole. Good, that, eh?"

"Medvegy's Cellar; that's in Budapest."

"In the spring, if you hang around the hotels—my dear sir," said Probka, "you'd be surprised at the things they throw away. Many's the leg of fowl I've got out of the dustbins in Budapest in the spring."

"Leg? Once I found a half a duck. I dusted it off a bit and there it was, like new. They've got so much, these people, they don't know what to do with it. So they chuck it in the dust hole. It had some sauce on it, too."

"I once found a whole chicken," said Probka.

"Yes? I once found a goose, a whole goose, in a copper pan."

"You lie," he said distinctly.

"Say that again."

"Bah." Probka uncorked the bottle. "I know a man who was in Berlin once, and so one day he happens to open up a dustbin and finds—guess what! A ham. I tell you, a whole ham, only a little bit off. But give me sausage.

"In the old days," said Probka, "I used to eat a lot of sausage, a kind of special sausage made with goose-fat and garlic."

"Millionaire," sneered Bicskas.

"I used to have a rag-and-bone business."

"You needn't try to come over me with your rag-and-bone business. I used to be chucker-out in the Café Cseh. I had a blue uniform. I nearly bought a watch."

"By God," said Probka, "it grows cold. I bet neither of us lives through the winter."

"I have also been a coachman. I had some proper boots then, I don't mind telling you."

"We ought to have a fire," said Probka.

"My master was a count. We had Arab horses."

"I used to drink hot brandy on cold nights. I could do with some now, by heaven I could. Do you know what happened here last winter?"

"What?"

"A woman was found frozen right here, with a newborn baby in her arms. She was a lady, too."

"Lady!"

"Yes, here she sat, blue and stiff, with this kid, not two hours old, dead in her arms."

"If she was a lady she wouldn't have been here. She'd be at home, by the fire, that's where she'd be."

"You wouldn't understand, friend Bicskas. Perhaps there was a disgrace. I've dealt with many a noble family, and I understand things like that."

"Remember the wolves?" said Bicskas. "The winter when the wolves came down here and they sent fifty soldiers to kill them off? *Snap-snap!* All they found next day was fifty rifles in the snow. Not even a bloodstain; they'd lapped it all up. They're devils, wolves."

"It was sixty soldiers."

"Fifty."

"I've been coming here for thirty years, so I ought to know."

"I've been here off and on for forty years."

"I can read and write," said Probka.

"I can read capital letters."

There was silence. Then Bicskas laughed and said, "The sun looks like blood."

"I ought to know what goes on round here," said Probka, offended. "It's house and home to me, this stone."

"Well, damn it, so it is to me, too. It's a *place*. 'Where now?' you say; and then you say, 'Let's go to the stone.' That's how it is."

"You can sit here, sleep here, talk here, eat here. It's a club. You can also write your name down. Then there's sort of *something*. I cut my name over there."

"I did not exactly cut my name," said Bicskas, "but I made a cross."

"Let us try to sleep," said Probka.

By daybreak four more tramps had come. There was a woman who did not resemble a woman, and a man who did not look like a man; there was a bundle of rags wrapped in an old sheepskin, that laughed and smoked, accompanied by his wife who sat in impenetrable silence. They rested, fitting their bones into the mossier indentations of the stone.

"But who is this who comes?" asked Bicskas, suddenly.

A train of carts, followed by a carriage, rolled slowly down the north fork of the road. The tramps, watching, saw that there were also men in uniform, riding horses.

A giant in blue and silver, with a mustache quite twelve inches from tip to tip, rode up to the stone, surveyed the tramps with a supercilious scowl, wrinkled his nose and said, "Off."

"Sir?" said Probka.

"Clear out."

Bicskas snarled.

"Off!" roared the giant with the mustache. The tramps dragged themselves away. Only Probka and Bicskas remained.

"We insist on our rights," said Probka. "This is our stone."

The horseman drew a revolver, and said, "Two seconds."

"If you shoot it's murder," said Probka.

"Get out!"

Probka went away. Bicskas followed him. From a distance they watched. The shapeless thing in the sheepskin, speaking for the first and last time, said, "I cut a *J*, for Janos, in the right-hand corner, with a horseshoe nail, for luck. And an *E* for Etelka. That's my old woman."

"They've brought up a crane," said Bicskas. "They're taking the stone away. By God! Let's . . ."

"Against guns?" said Probka. "I think they're only turning it over."

The woman who did not resemble a woman shrieked suddenly. "It moves!"

Slowly, encumbered by the weight of all its centuries, the stone moved. The earth cracked. Pale insects that lived out of the daylight writhed, terrified, back into the ground. The stone groaned. The crane groaned. The workmen shouted. The watchers held their breath. Probka prayed, "Oh God, let the chains break!"

But the chains held. The bottom of the stone became visible, black with earth. The tramps cried out. They felt in the soles of their feet the jolt of the huge stone teetering on end. A workman yelled, "Hold!" The stone stood, gently rocking. An old gentleman said, "Here. Now." Soon, having propped up the stone with beams, men began to dig. When night fell, flares were lit. The men dug till dawn. More men came with picks and spades. The waiting tramps, now fifty strong, muttered among themselves.

From out of the newly dug pit came a shout, "Eljen! Eljen!" It was a cry of triumph. The chains clanked again. Men groaned.

"Hup!" Strange objects were coming out of the ground into the light—dull, dirty pieces of armor; huge pots and troughs; battered cups; bent disks—masses of old, broken metal of unfamiliar shapes and unwieldy sizes.

Probka, bowing low before an armed guard, said, "Honored sir, be graciously pleased to tell me why this old iron was buried here."

"That is not old iron," said the guard. "That is pure gold. It is one of the treasures of the Scourge of God, Attila. It is worth God knows how many millions."

"And for seven hundred years we have been dying of hunger here," said Probka. Nothing more was said. Bitterness was too profound for expression. There were no words, even in the frightful vocabularies of the damned.

The tramps camped about the hole. When the diggers had gone away, they probed the pit with their fingers, hoping to find some forgotten coin or jewel. But they found nothing, except worms and stones, and a heavy smell as of the grave. And so, at last, they went their ways over the endless, wind-tattered plain; and although it covered a treasure the plainsmen still call the stone The Beggars' Stone, in spite of the fact that since it was disturbed no beggar has rested there.

THE BRIGHTON MONSTER

By 1943 the importance of old rags, bones, bottles and scraps of waste paper had been drummed into the head of England so thoroughly that salvage became a neurosis, a delirium, something like a disease. The British people were compelled to realize that waste cost lives. Merchant seamen risked everything in bringing to our shores cargoes of wood pulp, foodstuffs and metals. If you kept a book you did not need or burned a love letter, lost a hairpin, or threw an inch of potato peel into the wrong receptacle, you were made to feel that you had murdered a sailor. There was a formidable drive to round up hitherto unconsidered scraps—especially scraps of paper. The government offices, and even the secretive old-established lawyers of Bedford Row and the Temple let go their ancient, outdated documents. The authorities had solemnly promised that private papers would be shredded and pulped without being read.

In those brave days I was the war correspondent for *The People*. One afternoon, a little while before I went to join the American Ninth Air Force at Saint Jacques, I called at my office and found the passage blocked with bins and baskets and bundles of waste paper, put out for the salvage men. (For all I know to the contrary I am writing this on a re-hashed bit of that same paper). There were tens of thousands of letters, unclaimed typescripts, execrable poems in manuscript, usually in a feminine hand, stale cablegrams, musty galley proofs, preposterous books sent for review that were not worth selling or giving away . . . the inevitable papery detritus of an active but old-fashioned office.

I number among my weaknesses an incurable habit of rummaging among rubbish heaps. I must poke my fingers into everything. So I stirred the surface of the foremost basket and, having glanced at a letter on hand-made paper from a lord who had had a revelation of the end of the world, picked up an unbound, badly sewn pamphlet printed by Partridge of Paternoster Row in London, 1747.

Attached to it with a rusty paper clip was an unsigned, undated note, without an address, which said: *Dear Editor, I found this in my grandfather's Bible. Please make what use of it you like. I do not put my name and address because I do not want publicity. As a regular reader of your excellent paper for the last thirty years my desire is only to do you a good turn.* The writing was that of an old lady, probably rheumatic.

If she will get in touch with me, whoever she may be, I will gladly give her whatever I may be paid for this story, to spend as she thinks fit; because her little unbound pamphlet of 1747 links up with the most terrible event in history, to make the most remarkable story of our time.

The pamphlet, in itself, is nothing but a piece of pretentious nonsense written by one of those idle dabblers in natural philosophy (as they called it) who loved to rush into print at their own expense in the eighteenth and nineteenth centuries. They seem ridiculous now, with their pompous, Latin-sprinkled "philosophical" accounts of seaweed and thunderbolts, electricity and dephlogisticated air, amalgams and rhubarb.

Nearly everything then was "remarkable" or "extraordinary," especially living freaks. Lambert the fat man was a celebrity—simply because he was big; someone else became famous merely because he was a midget. The author of my pamphlet had attempted to tickle his way into the public notice with the feather of his pen by writing an account of a monster captured by a boatman fishing several miles out of Brighthelmstone in the County of Sussex in the summer of the year 1745.

The name of the author was the Reverend Arthur Titty. I see him as one of those pushing, self-assertive vicars of the period, a rider to hounds, a purple-faced consumer of prodigious quantities of old port; a man of independent fortune, trying to persuade the world and himself that he was a deep thinker and a penetrating observer of the mysterious works of

God. There is a sort of boozy, winey, slapdash repetitiveness in his style. Yet he must have been a man of considerable education: he spoke to his monster in Latin, Greek, Hebrew, French and Italian—not one word of which the monster understood. Also he could draw a little. *Titty, delin.*, is printed under the illustration.

I should never have taken the trouble to pocket the Reverend Arthur Titty's *Account of a Strange Monster Captured Near Brighthelmstone in the County of Sussex on August 6th in the Year of Our Lord 1745* if it had not been for the coincidence of the date: I was born on August 6th. So I pushed the yellowed, damp-freckled pages into the breast pocket of my battledress, and thought no more about them until April, 1947, when a casual remark sent me running, yelling like a maniac, to the cupboard in which my old uniforms were hanging.

The pamphlet was still in its pocket. I would not have lost that pamphlet for five hundred pounds.

I shall not waste your time or strain your patience with the Reverend Arthur Titty's turgid, high-falutin' prose or his references to *De rerum*—this that and the other. I propose to give you the unadorned facts in the very queer case of the Brighthelmstone Monster.

Brighthelmstone is now known as Brighton—a large, popular, prosperous holiday resort delightfully situated on the coast of Sussex by the Downs. But in the Reverend Arthur Titty's day no one had ever heard of the place. King George IV made it popular when he was Prince Regent. The air and the water were recommended by his medical adviser. His presence made Brighthelmstone fashionable, and popular usage shortened the name of the place. In 1745 it was an obscure village.

If a fisherman named Hodge had not had an unlucky night on August 5th, 1745, on the glass-smooth sea off Brighthelmstone, this story would never have been told. He had gone out with his brother-in-law, George Rodgers, and they had caught nothing but a few small and valueless fishes. Hodge was desperate. He was notorious in the village as a spendthrift and a drunkard and it was suspected that he had a certain connection with a barmaid at The Smack Inn—it was alleged that she had a child by Hodge in the spring of the following year. He had scored up fifteen shillings for beer and needed a new net. It is probable, therefore, that Hodge stayed out in his boat until after the dawn of August 6th because he feared to face his wife—who also, incidentally, was with child.

At last, glum, sullen and thoroughly out of sorts, he prepared to go home.

And then, he said, there was something like a splash—only it was not a splash: it was rather like the bursting of a colossal bubble; and there, in the sea, less than ten yards from his boat, was the monster, floating.

George Rodgers said, "By gogs, Jack Hodge, yon's a man!"

"Man? How can 'a be a man? Where could a man come from?"

The creature that had appeared with the sound of a bursting bubble drifted closer, and Hodge, reaching out with a boathook, caught it under the chin and pulled it to the side of the boat.

"That be a merman," he said, "and no Christian man. Look at 'un, all covered wi' snakes and firedrakes, and yellow like a slug's belly. By the Lord, George Rodgers, this might be the best night's fishing I ever did if it's alive, please the Lord! For if it is I can sell that for better money than ever I got for my best catch this last twenty years, or any other fisherman either. Lend a hand, Georgie-boy, and let's have a feel of it."

George Rodgers said, "That's alive, by hell—look now, and see the way the blood runs down where the gaff went home."

"Haul it in, then, and don't stand there gaping like a puddock."

They dragged the monster into the boat. It was shaped like a man and covered from throat to ankle with brilliantly colored images of strange monsters. A green, red, yellow and blue thing like a lizard sprawled between breastbone and navel. Great serpents were coiled about its legs. A smaller snake, red and blue, was pricked out on the monster's right arm: the snake's tail covered the forefinger and its head was hidden in the armpit. On the lefthand side of its chest there was a big heart-shaped design in flaming scarlet. A great bird like an eagle in red and green spread its wings from shoulder blade to shoulder blade, and a red fox chased six blue rabbits from the middle of his spine into some unknown hiding place between his legs. There were lobsters, fishes and insects on his left arm and on his right buttock a devilfish sprawled, encircling the lower part of his body with its tentacles. The back of his right hand was decorated with a butterfly in yellow, red, indigo and green. Low down, in the center of the throat, where the bone begins, there was a strange, incomprehensible, evil-looking symbol.

The monster was naked. In spite of its fantastic appearance it was so unmistakably a male human being that George Rodgers—a weak-minded but respectable man—covered it with a sack. Hodge prised open the monster's mouth to look at its teeth, having warned his brother-in-law to stand by with an ax in case of emergency. The man-shaped creature out of the sea had red gums, a red tongue and teeth as white as sugar.

They forced it to swallow a little gin—Hodge always had a flask of gin in the boat—and it came to life with a great shudder and cried out in a strange voice, opening wild black eyes and looking crazily left and right.

"Tie that up. You tie that's hands while I tie that's feet," said Hodge.

The monster offered no resistance.

"Throw 'un back," said George Rodgers, suddenly overtaken by a nameless dread. "Throw 'un back, Jack, I say!"

But Hodge said, "You be mazed, George Rodgers, you born fool. I can sell 'e for twenty-five golden guineas. Throw 'un back? I'll throw '*ee* back for a brass farthing, tha' witless fool!"

There was no wind. The two fishermen pulled for the shore. The monster lay in the bilge, rolling its eyes. The silly, good-natured Rodgers offered it a crust of bread which it snapped up so avidly that it bit his finger to the bone. Then Hodge tried to cram a wriggling live fish into its mouth, but "the Monster spat it out *pop*, like a cork out of a bottle, saving your Honor's presence."

Brighthelmstone boiled over with excitement when they landed. Even the Reverend Arthur Titty left his book and his breakfast, clapped on his three-cornered hat, picked up his clouded cane and went down to the fish-market to see what was happening. They told him that Hodge had caught a monster, a fish that looked like a man, a merman, a hypogriff, a sphinx—heaven knows what. The crowd parted, and Titty came face to face with the monster.

Although the monster understood neither Hebrew, Greek, Latin, Italian nor French, it was obvious that it was a human being, or something remarkably like one. This was evident in its manner of wrinkling its forehead, narrowing its eyes, and demonstrating that it was capable of understanding—or of wanting to understand, which is the same thing. But it could not speak; it could only cry out incoherently and was obviously greatly distressed, like a man paralyzed by horror in a nightmare. The Reverend Arthur Titty said, "Oafs, ignorant louts! This is no sea monster, you fools, no *lusus naturae*, but an unfortunate shipwrecked mariner."

According to the pamphlet, Hodge said, "Your Reverence, begging your Reverence's pardon, how can that be, since for the past fortnight there has been no breath of wind and no foreign vessel in these parts? If this be an unfortunate shipwrecked mariner, where is the wreck of his ship, and where was it wrecked? I have great respect for your Reverence's opinions, but I humbly ask your Reverence how he appeared as you might say out of a bubble without warning on the face of the water, floating. And if your Honor will take the trouble to observe this unhappy creature's skin your Reverence will see that it shows no signs of having been immersed for any considerable period in the ocean."

I do not imagine for a moment that this is what Hodge really said; he probably muttered the substance of the argument in the form of an angry protest emphasized by a bitten-off oath or two. However, the Reverend Arthur Titty perceived that what the fisherman said was "not without some show of reason" and said that he proposed to take the monster to his house for examination.

Hodge protested vigorously. It was his monster, he said, because he had caught it in the open sea with his own hands, in his own boat, and parson or no parson, if Titty were the Archbishop himself an Englishman had his rights. After some altercation, in the course of which the monster fainted, the Reverend Arthur Titty gave Hodge a silver crown piece for the loan of the monster for philosophical observation. They poured a few buckets of sea water over the monster, which came back to consciousness with a tremulous sigh. This was regarded as positive proof of its watery origin. Then it was carried to Titty's house on a hurdle.

It rejected salt water as a drink, preferring fresh water or wine, and ate cooked food, expressing, with unmistakable grimaces, a distaste for raw fish and meat. It was put to bed on a heap of clean straw and covered with a blanket which was kept moistened with sea water. Soon the Monster of Brighthelmstone revived and appeared desirous of walking. It could even make sounds reminiscent of human speech.

The Reverend Arthur Titty covered its nakedness under a pair of his old breeches and one of his old shirts . . . as if it had not been grotesque looking enough before.

He weighed it, measured it and blooded it to discover whether it was thick or thin blooded, cold or hot blooded. According to Titty's fussy little account the monster was about five feet one and three-quarter inches tall. It weighed exactly one hundred and nineteen pounds and walked upright. It possessed unbelievable strength and superhuman agility. On one occasion the Reverend Arthur Titty took it out for a walk on the end of a leather leash. The local blacksmith, one of Hodge's boon companions, who was notorious for his gigantic muscular power and bad temper—he was later to achieve nationwide fame as Clifford, who broke the arm of the champion wrestler of Yorkshire—accosted the Reverend Arthur Titty outside his smithy and said, "Ah, so that's Hodge's catch as you stole from him. Let me feel of it to see if it be real," and he pinched the monster's shoulder very cruelly with one of his great hands—hands that could snap horseshoes and twist iron bars into spirals. The inevitably attendant crowd of awestruck children and gaping villagers witnessed the event. The monster, baring big white teeth in a snarl of rage, moving with dazzling speed picked up the two-hundred-pound blacksmith and threw him into a heap of scrap iron three yards away. For an anxious second or two Titty thought that the monster was going to run amok, for its entire countenance changed; the nostrils quivered, the eyes shone with fierce intelligence, and from its open mouth there came a weird cry. Then the creature relapsed into heavy dejection and let itself be led home quietly, while the astonished blacksmith, bruised and bleeding, limped back to his anvil with the shocked air of a man who has seen the impossible come to pass.

Yet, the monster was an extremely sick monster. It ate little, sometimes listlessly chewing the same mouthful for fifteen minutes. It liked to squat on its haunches and stare unblinkingly at the sea. It was naturally assumed that it was homesick for its native element, and so it was soused at intervals with buckets of brine and given a large tub of sea water to sleep in if it so desired. A learned doctor of medicine came all the way from Dover to examine it and pronounced it human; unquestionably an air-breathing mammal. But so were whales and crocodiles breathers of air that lived in the water.

Hodge, alternately threatening and whimpering, claimed his property. The Reverend Arthur Titty called in his lawyer, who so bewildered the unfortunate fisherman with Latin quotations, legal jargon, dark hints and long words that, cursing and growling, he scrawled a cross in lieu of a signature at the foot of a document in which he agreed to relinquish all claim on the monster in consideration of the sum of seven guineas, payable on the spot. Seven guineas was a great deal of money for a fisherman in those days. Hodge had never seen so many gold pieces in a heap, and had never owned one. Still, the monster brought him bad luck in the end, and it would have been better for Hodge if he had gone home instead of loitering optimistically on the still sea that August morning. A traveling showman visited the Reverend Arthur Titty and offered him twenty-five guineas for the monster, which Titty refused. In the interests of natural philosophy, this monster was not for sale. The showman spoke of the matter in "The Smack," and Hodge, who had been drunk for a week, behaved "like one demented," as Titty wrote in a contemptuous footnote. He made a thorough nuisance of himself, demanding the balance of the twenty-five guineas which were his by rights, was arrested and fined for riotous conduct. Then he was put in the stocks as an incorrigible drunkard, and the wicked little urchins of Brighthelmstone threw fish guts at him. By this time his simple-minded brother-in-law Rodgers, egged on by Hodge's shrewish sister, had quarreled with him. Rodgers demanded half of the seven guineas. Hodge had given him only twelve shillings. Let out of the stocks with a severe reprimand, smelling horribly of dead fish, Hodge went to "The Smack" and ordered a quart of strong ale, which came in a heavy can. Rodgers came in for his modest morning draft, and told Hodge that he was nothing better than a damned rogue. Irritated to the verge of madness Hodge, having drunk his quart, struck Rodgers with the can, and broke his skull; for which he was hanged not long afterward.

So the Brighthelmstone Monster brought bad luck to poor Rodgers too.

The Reverend Arthur Titty, also, suffered because of the monster. After the killing of Rodgers and the hanging of Hodge the fishermen began to hate him. Heavy stones were thrown against his shutters at night. Someone set fire to one of his haystacks. This must have given Titty something to think about, for rick burning was a hanging matter, and one may as well hang for a parson as for a haystack. He made up his mind to go to London and live in polite, natural-philosophical circles. The fishermen hated the monster too. They regarded it as a sort of devil. But the monster did not care. It was languishing, dying of a mysterious sickness. Curious sores had appeared at various points on the monster's body; they began as little white bumps such as one gets from stinging nettles, and slowly opened and would not close. The looseness of the skin, now, lent the dragons and snakes and fishes a disgustingly lifelike look: as the monster breathed, they writhed. Doctors bled the monster. A veterinary surgeon poured melted pitch on the sores. The Reverend Arthur Titty kept it well soaked in sea water and locked it in a room, because it had shown signs of wanting to escape.

At last, nearly three months after its first appearance in Brighthelmstone, the monster escaped. An old manservant, Alan English, unlocked the door, in the presence of the Reverend Arthur Titty, in order to give the monster its daily mess of vegetables and boiled meat. As the key turned the door was flung open with such violence that English fell forward into the room—his hand was still on the doorknob—and the monster ran out, crying aloud in a high, screaming voice. The Reverend Arthur Titty caught it by the shoulder, whereupon he was whisked away like a leaf in the wind and lay stunned at the end of the passage. The monster ran out of the house. Three responsible witnesses—Rebecca West, Herbert George and Abraham Herris (or Harris)—saw it running toward the sea, stark naked, although a north-east wind was blowing. The two men ran after it, and Rebecca West followed as fast as she could. The monster's wide bare feet crunched on the shingle. It ran straight into the bitter water and began to swim, its arms and legs vibrating like the wings of an insect. Herbert George saw it plunge into the green heart of a great wave, and then the heavy rain fell like a curtain and the Brighthelmstone Monster was never seen again.

The monster had never spoken. In the later stages of its disease its teeth had fallen out. With one of these teeth—obviously a canine—it had scratched certain marks on the dark oak panels of the door of the room in which it was confined. These marks the Reverend Arthur Titty faithfully recorded, and reproduced in his pamphlet.

The Brighthelmstone fishermen said that the sea devil had

gone back where it belonged, down to the bottom of the sea to its palace built of the bones of lost Christian sailors. Sure enough, half an hour after the monster disappeared there was a terrible storm, and many seamen lost their lives. In a month or so Titty left Brighthelmstone for London. The city swallowed him. He published his pamphlet in 1746—a bad year for natural philosophy, because the ears of England were still full of the Jacobite Rebellion of '45.

Poor Titty! If he could have foreseen the real significance of the appearance of the Monster of Brighthelmstone he would have died happy . . . probably in a lunatic asylum.

In April, 1947 I had the good fortune to meet one of my oldest and dearest friends, a colonel in Intelligence who, for obvious reasons, must remain anonymous, although he is supposed to be in retirement now and wears civilian clothes—very plain civilian clothes, elegantly cut in the narrow-sleeved style of the late nineteen-twenties, and rather the worse for wear. He has not had occasion to buy a suit since 1930, and is one of the last men in London to wear one of Lock's little cocky gray-speckled bowler hats. The Colonel is in many ways a romantic character, something like Rudyard Kipling's Strickland Sahib who lifted the last veil and saw things that no other white man ever saw and lived to boast about. His face is the color of lawyers' red tape, curiously wrinkled—the skin has something of the excoriated, over-used appearance of an actor's skin. He has played many strange parts in his time, that formidable old warrior; and his quick black eyes, disturbingly Asiatic-looking under the slackly drooping eyelids, have seen more than you and I will ever see.

He never talks about his work. An Intelligence officer who talks ceases automatically to be an Intelligence officer. A good deal of his conversation is of sport, manly sport—polo, pig-sticking, cricket, rugby football, hunting and, above all, boxing and wrestling. I imagine that the Colonel, who has lived underground in disguise for so many years of his life, finds relief in the big wide-open games in which a man must meet his opponent face to face yet may, without breaking the rules, play quick tricks. At the age of forty-eight he boxed three rounds with the lightweight champion, who told him that he was wasting his time in the army. It is as well for us, though, that he stayed where he was; I am not at liberty to tell you why.

We were drinking coffee and smoking cigarettes after dinner in my flat and he was talking about Oriental wrestling. He touched on wrestling technique among the Afghans and in the Deccan, and spoke with admiration of Gama, the Western Indian wrestler, still a rock-crusher at an age when most men are shivering in slippers by the fire, who beat Zbyszko in ten seconds; remarked on a South-Eastern Indian named Patil who could knock a strong man senseless with the knuckle of his left thumb; and went on to Chinese wrestlers, especially Mongolians, who are tremendously heavy and powerful, and use their feet. A good French Canadian lumberjack (the Colonel said), accustomed to dancing on rolling logs in a rushing river, could do dreadful things with his legs and feet, like Lucien Pacaud, the Tiger of Quebec who, in a scissors hold, killed Big Ted Glass of Detroit. In certain kinds of wrestling size and weight were essential, said the Colonel. The Japanese wrestlers of the heavy sort—the ones that weighed three or four hundred pounds and looked like pigs—those big ones that started on all fours and went through a series of ritual movements; they had to be enormously heavy. In fact the heavier they were the better.

He did not find this amusing, although there were certain subtle points that a connoisseur could not possibly fail to appreciate.

"No, Gerald my lad, give me jujitsu. There is no one on earth who can defeat a Black Belt—except someone who takes him by surprise. A three-hundred-and-fifty-pound man catching a jujitsu man unawares and simply falling on him with all his weight would naturally put him out of action, just as if the roof fell in on him. Or again, a scientific boxer, getting a well-placed punch in first would put him out for the count. But the higher initiates had better be attacked from behind. In jujitsu the real adept develops such wonderful co-ordination of hand and eye that if he happens to be expecting it he can turn to his own advantage even the lightning punch of a wizard like Jimmy Wilde. He could give away eight stone to Joe Louis and make him look silly. Of course, strictly speaking, it wouldn't be fair. The opponents would be attacking or defending along different lines. Georges Hackenschmidt, for instance, was one of the greatest catch-as-catch-can wrestlers that ever lived, and one of the strongest men of his day. But I ask you: would he, wrestling Catch, have stood up against Yukio Otani using jujitsu? Oh, by the way, speaking of Yukio Otani, did you ever hear of a Japanese wrestler called Sato?"

"I can't say that I have. Why? Should I have heard of him?"

"No, of course not. I have been so long out there that I tend to forget. You know, if I could only find that little fellow I might be a rich man yet. I always wanted to buy a nice little boat and go cruising around the Greek islands. A fat chance, on my wretched pay! And I sunk most of my savings in that wretched fellow Benny North, fool that I was. You remember that lout? I thought I'd discovered a real British heavyweight at last and as it turned out the damned fellow had a weak heart. No more heavyweights for me."

"What has this to do with Sato?"

"Why, he is, or was, a phenomenon. I think he was a better wrestler than Otani. My idea was to take him all round the world and challenge all comers—boxers, wrestlers, even fencers, to stand up against him for ten minutes. He was unbelievable. Furthermore, he looked so frightful. I won a hundred and fifty quid on him at Singapore in 1938. He took on four of the biggest and best boxers and wrestlers we could lay our hands on and floored the whole lot in eleven minutes by the clock. Just a minute, I've got a picture in my wallet. I keep it because it looks so damn funny. Look."

The Colonel handed me a dog-eared photograph of an oddly assorted group. There was a hairy mammoth of a man, obviously a wrestler, standing with his arms folded so that his biceps looked like coconuts, by the side of another man, almost as big, but with the scrambled features of a rough-and-tumble bruiser. There was one blond grinning man who looked like a light heavyweight, and a beetle-browed middleweight with a bulldog jaw. The Colonel was standing in the background, smiling in a fatherly way. In the foreground smiling into the camera stood a tiny Japanese. The top of his head was on a level with the big wrestler's breastbone, but he must have measured at least two feet six inches across the shoulders—he was more than half as broad as he was tall. He was all chest and arms. The knuckles of his closed hands touched his knees. I took the picture to the light and looked more closely. The photographer's flash-bulb had illuminated every detail. Sato had made himself even more hideous with tattooing. He was covered with things that creep and crawl, real and fabulous. A dragon snarled on his stomach. Snakes were coiled about his legs. Another snake wound itself about his right arm from forefinger to armpit. The other arm was covered with angry looking lobsters and goggle-eyed fishes, and on the left breast there was the conventionalized shape of a heart.

It was then that I uttered an astonished oath and went running to look for my old uniform, which I found, with the Reverend Arthur Titty's pamphlet still in the inside breast pocket. The Colonel asked me what the devil was the matter with me. I smoothed out the pamphlet and gave it to him without a word.

He looked at it, and said: "How very extraordinary!" Then he put away his eyeglass and put on a pair of spectacles; peered intently at the Reverend Arthur Titty's painstaking drawing of the Brighthelmstone Monster, compared it with the photograph of Sato and said to me, "I have come across some pretty queer things in my time, but I'm damned if I know what to make of this."

"What sort of tattooing did your Sato have on his back?" I asked.

He replied, without hesitation, "A crimson and emerald-green hawk stooping between the shoulders and a foxy red fox chasing six bluey-green rabbits down his backbone; an octopus on the right buttock throwing out the tentacles around groin and belly—very clever piece of work—must have hurt him like the devil."

"Look here," I said pointing to the relevant passage in the pamphlet.

My friend the Colonel will swear horribly over trivialities. But when he is deeply moved he says: "Well! Really!" He said it now.

"But wait a minute," I said. "This Brighton Monster scratched something on the door. The old Reverend took a copy of it. Turn over four or five pages and you'll see it there, I think."

The Colonel looked at the copied marks scratched by the monster with one of its own teeth on the door of its cell. The spongy old paper was crumpled and cracked, and the marks were blurred by time, and by the dampness of lumber rooms and the moisture of my body. He looked at them, found a piece of paper and a pencil, laid the paper against a wall, and copied the inscription, holding the pencil half an inch from the point. When he turned, I saw that the red of his face had faded to grayish pink.

"Well?" I said.

"Little Sato had been baptized, you know. He was a Christian, among other things. I don't know if I mentioned it."

"No, you didn't. Why?"

"Why, this says: *I was asleep with my wife. It was all a bad dream. Now I know that it was not a dream. God have mercy on poor Sato who must die. Hiroshima 1945.* How can it be? Sato had a wife, and they lived somewhere in Hiroshima. . . . He was in the Jap navy—submarines—and he *was* on leave in August, 1945, when they dropped that damned thing which I wish to God they'd never thought of. I don't understand this. There must be a mistake somewhere. Yet this is Sato all right. What do you make of it? This beats me. I suppose, of course, poor little Sato got it when we dropped that confounded atom bomb. But—"

"I never was in favor of fiddling about with atoms," I said, "it always seemed to me that there is a limit to what one ought to know. All those fantastic blasts and horrible disintegrations! One feels like the sorceror's apprentice! You will observe, by the way, that this wretched Brighton Monster suffered from peculiar cancerous sores?"

The Colonel said: "Poor Sato! I liked the little fellow. But my dear Kersh, I hate to think what I can't help thinking. To die, that's nothing. It's easier to die than to live, once you get the hang of it. But this nasty business—it seems to indicate that you *don't* actually die when you run into one of those damned things. That was Sato, without a doubt. But imagine it—just imagine it! I don't believe I ever mentioned that I was married once? You go to sleep happily, and then . . . Poor little Sato! Flipped back two hundred years. Or it might be forward two hundred years . . . Of course the earth turns and space shifts. He might have found himself in the middle of the Sahara Desert, or at the South Pole, or in some place where they'd worship him like a god straight out of heaven. But Kersh, Kersh, think of the horror of it! The nightmare—you were asleep—that turns out to be no nightmare at all. You wake up, with a sigh of relief, and there is your nightmare still. The loneliest death imaginable! Can you wonder at poor Sato's despair? A Jap will kill himself as soon as look at you. So he ran out and threw himself into the sea. . . . How cold it must have been for him in Brighton in November!"

So, out of a salvage basket on the third floor of No. 93 Long Acre, London, W.C. 2 came the only evidence of a double death —the unique history of a man unhappily destined to be a victim of natural philosophy twice in two hundred years.

Here is food for thought, but I do not like the thought it feeds.

THE EXTRAORDINARILY HORRIBLE DUMMY

An uneasy conviction tells me that this story is true, but I hate to believe it. It was told to me by Ecco, the ventriloquist, who occupied a room next to mine in Busto's apartment house. I hope he lied. Or perhaps he was mad? The world is so full of liars and lunatics that one never knows what is true and what is false.

All the same, if ever a man had a haunted look that man was Ecco. He was small and furtive. He had disturbing habits; five minutes of his company would have set your nerves on edge. For example, he would stop in the middle of a sentence, say *Ssh!* in a compelling whisper, look timorously over his shoulder and listen to something. The slightest noise made him jump. Like all Busto's tenants, he had come down in the world. There had been a time when he topped bills and drew fifty pounds a week. Now, he lived by performing to theatre queues.

And yet he was the best ventriloquist I have ever heard. His talent was uncanny. Repartee cracked back and forth without pause, and in two distinct voices. There were even people who swore that his dummy was no dummy, but a dwarf or a small boy with painted cheeks, trained in ventriloquial back-chat. But this was not true. No dummy was ever more palpably stuffed with sawdust. Ecco called it Micky; and his act, "Micky and Ecco."

All ventriloquists' dummies are ugly, but I have yet to see one uglier than Micky. It had a home-made look. There was something disgustingly avid in the stare of its bulging blue eyes, the lids of which clicked as it winked; and an extraordinarily horrible ghoulishness in the smacking of its great, grinning, red wooden lips. Ecco carried Micky with him wherever he went, and even slept with it. You would have felt cold at the sight of Ecco, walking upstairs, holding Micky at arm's length. The dummy was large and robust; the man was small and wraithlike; and in a bad light you would have thought: *The dummy is leading the man!*

I said he lived in the room next to mine. But in London you may live and die in a room, and the man next door may never know. I should never have spoken to Ecco but for his habit of practicing ventriloquism by night. It was nerve-racking. At the best of times it was hard to find rest under Busto's roof; but Ecco made nights hideous, really hideous. You know the shrill, false voice of the ventriloquist's dummy? Micky's voice was not like that. It was shrill, but querulous; thin, but real—not Ecco's voice distorted, but a *different* voice. You would have sworn that there were two people quarreling. *This man is good*, I thought. Then: *But this man is perfect!* And at last, there crept into my mind this sickening idea: *There are two men!*

In the dead of night, voices would break out:

"Come on, try again!"

"I can't!"

"You must—"

"I want to go to sleep."

"Not yet; try again!"

"I'm tired, I tell you; I can't!"

"And I say try again."

Then there would be peculiar singing noises, and at length Ecco's voice would cry:

"You devil! You devil! Let me alone, in the name of God!"

One night, when this had gone on for three hours I went to Ecco's door, and knocked. There was no answer. I opened the door. Ecco was sitting there, gray in the face, with Micky on his knee. "Yes?" he said. He did not look at me, but the great painted eyes of the dummy stared straight into mine.

I said, "I don't want to seem unreasonable, but this noise . . ."

Ecco turned to the dummy and said, "We're annoying the gentleman. Shall we stop?"

Micky's dead red lips snapped as he replied, "Yes. Put me to bed."

Ecco lifted him. The stuffed legs of the dummy flapped lifelessly as the man laid him on the divan and covered him with a blanket. He pressed a spring. *Snap!* the eyes closed. Ecco drew a deep breath and wiped sweat from his forehead.

"Curious bedfellow," I said.

"Yes," said Ecco. "But . . . please—" And he looked at Micky, frowned at me and laid a finger to his lips. "Ssh!" he whispered.

"How about some coffee?" I suggested.

He nodded. "Yes, my throat is very dry," he said. I beckoned. That disgusting stuffed dummy seemed to charge the atmosphere with tension. He followed me on tiptoe and closed his door silently. As I boiled water on my gas-ring I watched him. From time to time he hunched his shoulders, raised his eyebrows and listened. Then, after a few minutes of silence, he said suddenly, "You think I'm mad."

"No," I said, "not at all; only you seem remarkably devoted to that dummy of yours."

"I hate him," said Ecco; and listened again.

"Then why don't you burn the thing?"

"For God's sake!" cried Ecco, and clasped a hand over my mouth. I was uneasy—it was the presence of this terribly nervous man that made me so. We drank our coffee, while I tried to make conversation.

"You must be an extraordinarily fine ventriloquist," I said.

"Me? No, not very. My father, yes. He was great. You've heard of Professor Vox? Yes, well he was my father."

"Was he, indeed?"

"He taught me all I know; and even now . . . I mean . . . without him, you understand—nothing! He was a genius. Me, I could never control the nerves of my face and throat. So you see, I was a great disappointment to him. He . . . well, you know; he could eat a beefsteak, while Micky, sitting at the same table, sang *Je crois entendre encore*. That was genius. He used to make me practice, day in and day out—*Bee, Eff, Em, En, Pe, Ve, Doubleyou*, without moving the lips. But I was no good. I couldn't do it. I simply couldn't. He used to give me hell. When I was a child, yes, my mother used to protect me a little. But afterward! Bruises—I was black with them. He was a terrible man. Everybody was afraid of him. You're too young to remember: he looked like—well, look."

Ecco took out a wallet and extracted a photograph. It was brown and faded, but the features of the face were still vivid. Vox had a bad face; strong but evil—fat, swarthy, bearded and forbidding. His huge lips were pressed firmly together under a heavy black mustache, which grew right up to the sides of a massive flat nose. He had immense eyebrows, which ran together in the middle; and great, round, glittering eyes.

"You can't get the impression," said Ecco, "but when he came out to the stage in a black cloak lined with red silk, he looked just like the devil. He took Micky with him wherever he went—they used to talk in public. But he was a great ventriloquist—the greatest ever. He used to say, 'I'll make a ventriloquist of you if it's the last thing I ever do.' I had to go with him wherever he went, all over the world; and stand in the wings and watch him; and go home with him at night and practice again—*Bee*, *Eff*, *Em*, *En*, *Pe*, *Ve*, *Doubleyou*—over and over again, sometimes till dawn. You'll think I'm crazy."

"Why should I?"

"Well . . . This went on and on, until—*ssh*—did you hear something?"

"No, there was nothing. Go on."

"One night I . . . I mean, there was an accident. I—he fell down the elevator shaft in the Hotel Dordogne, in Marseilles. Somebody left the gate open. He was killed." Ecco wiped sweat from his face. "And that night I slept well, for the first time in my life. I was twenty years old then. I went to sleep, and slept well. And then I had a horrible dream. He was back again, see? Only not he, in the flesh; but only his voice. And he was saying: 'Get up, get up and try again, damn you; get up I say—I'll make a ventriloquist of you if it's the last thing I ever do. Wake up!'

"I woke up. You will think I'm mad.

"I swear. I still heard the voice; and it was coming from . . ."

Ecco paused and gulped.

I said, "Micky?" He nodded. There was a pause; then I said, "Well?"

"That's about all," he said. "It was coming from Micky. It has been going on ever since; day and night. He won't let me alone. It isn't I who makes Micky talk. Micky makes me talk. He makes me practice still . . . day and night. I daren't leave him. He might tell the . . . he might . . . oh God; anyway, I can't leave him . . . I can't."

I thought, *This poor man is undoubtedly mad. He has got the habit of talking to himself, and he thinks*—

At that moment I heard a voice; a little, thin, querulous, mocking voice, which seemed to come from Ecco's room. It said:

"Ecco!"

Ecco leaped up, gibbering with fright. "There!" he said. "There he is again. I must go. Forgive me. I'm not mad; not really mad. I must—"

He ran out. I heard his door open and close. Then there came again the sound of conversation, and once I thought I heard Ecco's voice, shaking with sobs, saying: *Bee, Eff, Em, En, Pe, Ve, Doubleyou* . . .

He is crazy, I thought; *yes, the man must be crazy . . . And before, he was throwing his voice . . . calling himself . . .*

But it took me two hours to convince myself of that; and I left the light burning all night, and I swear to you that I have never been more glad to see the dawn.

FANTASY OF A HUNTED MAN

In Kentucky, in the year 1918, there lived a ferocious old man who was known as the Major. I suppose he was of the kind that carves out empires and breaks open new territories. He was indomitable, wiry, strong as steel in spite of his sixty years, and devoid of fear. An admirable, though far from lovable man, he lived alone, deeply respected and half feared by everybody who knew him. He was something of a madman, terrifying in his fanatical devotion to anything he regarded as his duty. The Major belonged to the hard old days when men, single-handed, fought wildernesses and beat them tame.

Into his battered, lion-like head, there had crept the craziness of race-hate. He loathed foreigners, and abhorred Negroes, and was always to be found in the forefront of any demonstration against the unhappy black men of Kentucky—a figure of terror, with his rifle, and his great mustache which curved down like a sharp sickle, and his huge and glaring blue eyes.

That kind of fanaticism seems to bubble dangerously near the surface of the Deep South. A word cracks the skin over it, and lets loose an eruption of murder and cruelty.

One day, a hysterical woman said that she had been accosted by a Negro named Prosper. He had, in fact, asked her some question pertaining to firewood; but she had run, screaming for help. (That happens frequently.) She ran, I say, screaming. The drowsy little town seemed to start and blink. The Negroes knew what that meant and they trembled. Somebody passed a word to Prosper. He knew that innocence was no argument: he was a Negro black as night and therefore damned before judgment. He took to the woods, flying from what he knew must come.

A great mutter rose. Men clustered, tense and angry. Mouths twitched up in snarls. Beware of the undercurrent of bloodlust that crawls in the depths of men! Somebody yelled, "Are we going to let that nigra get away with this?" A hundred other voices roared: "No!" The mutter of the mob became a howl, like that of mad dogs. Guns came down from hooks. Night had fallen. Torches flared. Two great bloodhounds, straining at their leashes, snuffled on the trail of Prosper. The men followed the dogs. The mob was out for blood and torture. And the Major led them, with a gun loaded with buckshot under his arm.

But Prosper had a long start and he knew the woods. The mob hunted all night long and far into the next day. Then they became exhausted, and paused. But not the Major. He was drunk with hate. When everybody rested, he went on alone. He plunged into the depths of the wood. His long legs had the loping stride of a hunting wolf. The trees covered him. He disappeared.

And two days later he appeared again, and it seemed that he had gone quite mad. He was afraid! He cringed. He staggered toward some people who were watching him, and said, "I didn't do it! I never done nothing! I'm a harmless old nigger! Don't hurt me, white folks! Please don't hurt me!"

Then he fell into a sleep, so deep that it was almost a death. And when he awoke, twelve hours afterward, he was the Major again . . . but changed. He was quiet and gentle. He blinked uncertainly—he who had never been uncertain of anything, right or wrong, in sixty years of life—he who had never uttered a kind word in living memory. The Major, the nigger-hater, the lynch-lawyer, the whipper, the killer—the Major was seen gently patting the head of a terrified little black boy who stood, paralyzed with fear under the unexpected caress.

What had happened to him in that dark forest?

One day he told the story:

When the others had rested he had gone on, and on, until he could walk no longer. His body was exhausted, but not his hate. He determined to rest a little and then continue his hunt for the vanished Negro Prosper. And as he sat resting, sleep came down on him like a deadfall, and he lay among the leaves and snored.

But it was no ordinary sleep. It was a strange kind of sick coma in which the Major found himself. He was caught in the meshes of a dark and nightmarish dream, like a bird in a net. He knew that he was dreaming and struggled to awake, but could not. And then he found himself floating away . . . and there was a blank, a hiatus, a timeless silence.

He awoke. He found himself crouching in a thicket, in a part of the wood which he did not know. And his heart was thumping in his breast, and he was terrified, disgustingly terrified of something that was following him. The Major was bewildered. He had never known fear, and now he was afraid. He somehow knew that he was going to a hollow beyond the thicket. Something was urging him there. He knew, also, that dawn was at hand, and he dreaded the dawn . . . and yet he also dreaded the dark.

He had lost his rifle. His clothes seemed to have been torn to shreds by thorns. His face was swollen where branches had snapped back at him in his headlong rush through the wood.

He crawled on, footsore and exhausted. Prosper!—he had to find Prosper the Negro and drag him back to be slaughtered by the mob. But of what was he afraid? He did not know. The Major went on. He got out of the thicket. There, sure enough, dimly outlined in the starlight, lay a hut. He went toward it. It was a mere ruin. Those who had lived there had either died or gone away. It was empty.

He went in. He shouted, "Anybody here?"—and was surprised to hear the husky rasp of his voice. His throat was dry. He felt ill and weak . . . and still frightened. His mind revolted against the trembling of his limbs. His body was scared and wanted to hide. As he stood in the hut, shaking like a man in an ague, the first glimmer of day showed holes in his boots ". . . I must have been walking in black mud . . ." Then he saw his hands. They were black and wrinkled, with whitish nails and pink palms—Negro's hands.

Sick with anguish, the Major leaped up. There was a fragment of broken mirror. He looked at his reflection.

The terrified face of Prosper the Negro looked back at him.

He does not know how long he stood there, staring. He, the Major, was in the body of Prosper, the black fugitive. Some strange flash of intuition told him that somehow . . . God knew how . . . while he lay in his exhausted trance, and while Prosper also lay in a coma of weariness and misery . . . somehow their souls in sleep had met and changed places . . .

He heard, in the remote distance, a baying of bloodhounds.

The spirit of the Major turned to give battle. But the body of Prosper fainted with horror.

And it must have been exactly at that moment that the body of the Major, gibbering in the voice of Prosper, came staggering through the trees toward the lynch mob and begged for mercy, so that they took him home while the Negro escaped.

And then came the darkness of unconsciousness, out of which the Major struggled to find himself in his bed, surrounded by curious eyes and astonished faces.

That is all. There is only one thing more. The Major went into the wood again, and followed the route he remembered. There was the thicket; and there, in a hollow, lay the hut.

On the floor of the hut, smashed to pieces where it had been violently flung down, lay the remains of a bit of mirror.

THE GENTLEMAN ALL IN BLACK

There is a crazy old fellow who lives—or used to live, in 1937—in a crazy old skylight room in Paris, and was known as Le Borgne. He squinted horribly, and was well known for his avarice. Although he was reputed to have a large sum of money put by, he shuffled about in the ragged remains of a respectable black suit and tried to earn a few coppers doing odd jobs in cafés. He was not above begging . . . a very unsightly, disreputable, ill-tempered old man. And this is the story he told me one evening when he was trying to get two francs out of me.

"You needn't look down on me," he said. (He adopted a querulous, bullying tone even when asking a favor.) "I have been as well-dressed as you. I'm eighty years old, too. Ah yes, I have seen life, I have. Why, I used to be clerk to one of the greatest financiers in the world, no less a man than Mahler. That was before your time. That was fifty years ago. Mahler handled millions. I used to receive the highest of the high, the greatest of the great, in his office. There was no staff but me. Mahler worked alone, with me to write the letters. All his business was finished by three in the afternoon. He was a big man, and I was his right hand. I have met royalty in the office of Mahler. Why, once, yes, I even met the Devil."

And when I laughed at him, Le Borgne went on, with great vehemence:

Mahler died rich. And yet it is I who can tell you that a week before his death things went wrong and Mahler was nearly twenty million francs in debt. In English money, a million pounds, let us say. I was in his confidence. He had lost everything and, gambling in a mining speculation, had lost twenty million francs which were not his to lose. He said to me—it was on the 19th, or the 20th of April, 1887—"Well, Charles, it looks as if we are finished. I have nothing left except my immortal soul; and I'd sell that if I could get the worth of it." And then he went into his office.

I was copying a letter to the Bank, about five minutes later, when a tall, thin gentleman dressed all in black came into my room and asked to see Monsieur Mahler. He was a strange, foreign-looking gentleman, in a frock-coat of the latest cut and a big black cravat which hid his shirt. All his clothes were brand new, and there was a fine black pearl in his tie. Even his gloves were black. Yet he did not look as if he was in mourning. There was a power about him. I could not tell him that Mahler could not be disturbed. I asked him what name, and he replied, with a sweet smile: "Say—a gentleman." I had no time to announce him; I opened Mahler's door and this stranger walked straight in and shut the door behind him.

I used to listen to what went on. I put my ear to the door and listened hard, for this man in black intrigued me. And so I heard a very extraordinary conversation. The man in black spoke in a fine deep voice with an educated accent, and he said:

"Mahler, you are finished."

"Nonsense," said Mahler.

"Mahler, there is no use in your trying to deceive me. I can tell you positively that you are in debt to the tune of just over twenty million francs—to be exact, 20,002,907 francs. You have gambled, and have lost. Do you wish me to give you further details of your embezzlements?"

Calm as ice, Mahler said, "No. Obviously, you are in the know. Well, what do you want?"

"To help you."

At this Mahler laughed, and said, "The only thing that can help me is a draft on, say, Rothschild's, for at least twenty millions."

"I have more than that in cash," said the gentleman in black and I heard something fall heavily on Mahler's desk, and Mahler's cry of surprise.

"There are twenty-five millions there," said the stranger.

Mahler's voice shook a little as he replied, "Well?"

"Now let us talk. Monsieur Mahler, you are a man of the world, an educated man. Do you believe in the immortality of the soul?"

"Why, no," said Mahler.

"Good. Well, I have a proposition to make to you."

"But who are you?" Mahler asked.

"You'll know that soon enough. I have a proposition. Let us say that I am a buyer of men's time, men's lives. In effect, I buy men's souls. But let us not speak of souls. Let us talk in terms of time, which we all understand. I will give you twenty million francs for one year of your life—one year in which you must devote yourself utterly to me."

A pause: then Mahler said, "No." (Ah, he was a cunning man of business, poor Mahler!) "No. That is too long. It's too cheap at that price. I've made fifty million in less than a year before now."

I heard another little thud. The stranger said, "All right my friend. Fifty million francs."

"Not for a year," said Mahler.

The stranger laughed. "Then six months," he said.

And now I could tell, by the tone of his voice, that Mahler had taken control of the situation, for he could see that the strange man in black really wanted to buy his time. And Mahler had a hard, cold head, and was a genius at negotiation. Mahler said, "Not even one month."

Somehow, this affair brought sweat out on my forehead. It was too crazy. Mahler must have thought so too. The stranger said:

"Come. Do not let us quarrel about this. I buy time—any quantity of time, upon any terms. Time, my friend, is God's one gift to man. Now tell me, how much of your time, all the time that is yours, will you sell to me for fifty million?"

And the cold, even voice of Mahler replied, "Monsieur. You buy a strange commodity. Time is money. But *my* time is worth more money than most. Consider. Once, when Salomon Gold Mines rose twenty points overnight, I made something like twenty million francs by saying one word, *Soit*, which took half a second. *My* time, at that rate, is worth forty million a second, and two thousand four hundred million francs a minute. Now think of it like that—"

"Very well," said the visitor, quite unmoved. "I'll be even more generous. Fifty million a second. Will you sell me one second of your time?"

"Done," said Mahler.

The gentleman in black said, "Put the money away. Have no fear; it is real. And now I have bought one second of your time."

Silence for a little while. Then they both walked to the window, which was a first-floor one, and I heard the stranger say:

"I have bought one second of your time for fifty million francs. Ah well. Look down at all those hurrying people, my friend. That busy street. I am very old, and have seen much of men. Why, Monsieur Mahler . . . once, many years ago, I offered a man all the kingdoms of the earth. He would not take them. Yet in the end he got them. And I stood with him on a peak, and said to him what I say to you now—*Cast thyself down!*"

Silence. Then I seemed to come out of a sleep. The door of Mahler's office was open. Nobody was there. I looked out of the open window. There was a crowd. Mahler was lying in the street, sixteen feet below, with a broken neck. I have heard that a body falls exactly sixteen feet in precisely one second. That gentleman all in black was gone. I never saw him go. They said I had been asleep and dreamed him, and that Mahler had fallen by accident. Yet in Mahler's desk lay fifty million francs in bonds, which I had never seen there before. I am sure he never had them before. I believe, simply, that the gentleman in black was the Devil, and that he bought Mahler's soul. Think I am crazy if you like. On my mother's grave I swear that what I have told you is true. . . . And now can you give me fifty centimes? I want to buy a meal. . . ."

THE EYE

The generosity of the criminal generally consists in the giving away of something that never was, or no longer is, his own property. A case in point is that of the robber and murderer, Rurik Duncan, whose brief career was bloody, fierce and pitiless, but whose last empty gesture was thick and sticky with sentiment which uplifted the heart of a nation. Duncan gave away his eyes to be delivered after his death. It was regarded as a vital act of charity—in effect, a ticket to Salvation—that this singularly heartless fellow gave permission for his eyes to be grafted onto some person or persons unknown.

Similar cases have been printed in the newspapers. As it is with most philanthropists who give their all, so it was with this man Duncan. Having no further need for what he donated, he made a virtue of relinquishing it—stealing from his own grave, conning to the bitter end. I knew a billionaire whose ears were stopped during his lifetime against any plea for charity; but who, when his claws relaxed in death, gave what he had to orphans. I knew a Snow Maiden of an actress whose body is bequeathed to Science—whatever that may be. Rurik will rank with these, no doubt, on the Everlasting Plane. And why not? All the billionaire had that he was proud of was certain sums of money and holdings in perpetuity, which he let go because he had to. All the actress had was something of merely anatomical interest. Rurik had his eyes. He prized these eyes, which were of a strange, flecked, yellowish color. He could expand or contract them at will, and seemed to look in a different direction while he was watching your every movement.

Before we proceed with this old story, I had better make some kind of resumé of Rurik's career. He was born between the rocks and the desert, and was what, in my day, was called a "nuisance," but what is now termed a "juvenile delinquent."

In my day physical force used to be applied to such, whereafter they generally lived to die in their beds; now they bring in psychologists, and quite right, too, because you can never tell where anything begins or ends. It is only in extreme cases that a Rurik, nowadays, is stopped in his career with a tingling jolt and—first and last restraint—the pressure of certain heavy leather straps.

In brief: Rurik killed chickens, maimed sheep, corrupted and led a mob of fourteen-year-old muggers; graduated to the rackets in which he was employed to his pleasure and profit in nineteen states of the Union; got hot, gathered about him two coadjutors and became one of the most formidable operators since Dillinger. He had extraordinary luck, and a really remarkable sense of timing—without which no bank robber can hope to succeed. Also he had a highly developed administrative capacity, a strategic knack coupled with what one of the reporters called "tactical know-how." He could time a getaway to that split second in which a traffic light winks, letting a town throw up its own road-block. Rurik went plundering from bank to bank. It has been argued that with such superb dissimulation and timing he might have been a great actor or, perhaps, a great boxer. He might have been a copper baron, or oil king, or a banker, if only he had been born in the right place and at the right time; or literate, an ink-slinger. But he wasn't. He was born on an eroded farm, and went with a certain brilliance to his convulsive end.

Oddly enough, Rurik was not given to vindictiveness or hate, in the generally accepted sense of these terms. Something was missing from him that makes society possible. Call it a soul, call it a heart, call it pity; but say that he wanted to be alone. And so he was, right to the end, with a high-backed chair all to himself, and a secret which he thought he would carry on his own, looked within himself, to a narrow place where nobody could touch him.

This secret was the whereabouts of certain buried treasure; I mean the location of $2,600,000 which he had stolen and hidden nobody knew where.

It was Rurik who stole the armored truck in Butte, Montana. At any moment now the pulp-writers will rehash the Rurik snatch as a "perfect crime." The details are available in the files of all the newspapers in the world. It is sufficient to say, here, simply that Rurik and his two companions, later to be known as "The Unholy Three," exquisitely timing and balancing the operation, got away with an immense payroll, together with nearly all the money that had been in the vault of a great bank, one day, and seemed to evaporate, truck and all. *Timing, timing, timing,* said the Sunday supplement criminologists; until one became sick and tired of the word. There was also some reference to Mr. G.K. Chesterton's "The Invisible Man," whose cloak of invisibility was the fact that he was too familiar, at a given hour, to appear conspicuously out of place.

Both schools of thought were right: the timers and the psychologists. At one moment there was an armored truck loaded with money. Next moment there were three or four bewildered men, loosely holding pistols they did not know what to point at; three streets full of traffic had stopped for the lights, and a great fortune was on its way to nowhere. Only one shot was fired, and that by a bank guard named Larkin, a retired police officer who, when the three bandits appeared, one of them with a gun in his hand, let fly with a short-barreled .38. As it later transpired, Larkin hit Rurik in the hip and so precipitated his capture. When the money is recovered, it is believed, Larkin will have good legal grounds for claiming a reasonable portion of the reward. The robbers, by arrangement, carried unloaded automatics—it seems that Rurik was very particular about this. So, in about as long as it takes a man to say: "Was that a backfire?"—one of the greatest robberies of our time was perpetrated, and there was great federal perplexity. Anywhere in the world a man can disappear, as Willie Sutton did, simply by being patient and keeping still. In Montana, even an armored truck can disappear. But how does two and a half million-odd dollars disappear?

They found the truck a certain distance out of town, empty. Where, then, was the paper money and the silver?

Any moving-man will tell you that there is nothing heavier than paper, and any bank messenger will tell you that there is nothing more unwieldy than a bag of loose coin. He would be a very strong man indeed who could carry on his back even a quarter of a million dollars in small bills for the distance of fifteen city blocks. Throw in a bag or two of silver dollars to joggle the equilibrium, and put soft sand underfoot instead of paving stones, and no man can do it. A mule couldn't. And here not two hundred and fifty thousand, but two and a half million dollars had been spirited away to some hiding place in the rocks!

Reconstructing the affair, the federal authorities arrived at the conclusion that Rurik and his men stopped the truck somewhere on the outskirts of Butte and hid the money in some place tantalizingly close to town, known only to themselves. Each took $8,000 for current expenses. The truck was driven about fifteen miles further, to a point near where Rurik had hidden a getaway car. Rurik took this car, and then they separated, arranging to meet when it was expedient to do so. But this is what happened: Little Dominic, trying to buy a used car in Helena, was recognized and died fighting it out with the state troopers. MacGinnis lost his way northward among the rocks and died there, in his pig-headed way, rather than give himself up. Only Rurik was taken alive, having fainted through loss of blood in a filling-station.

It is worthy of note that before he lost consciousness, his last words were: "Even maps you can't trust," and afterward raved of the illusion of space and the fallacy of distance, until they brought him to. The State pumped into Rurik the solid blood and the plasma of I forget how many honest men before he was brought to trial and convicted of the bank robbery. Here the FBI furnished the additional information that, under another name, Rurik was wanted in the state of New York for murder. So he was shipped back to New York, neatly patched up, and there after fair trial, found guilty and sentenced to death by electrocution. He took the sentence impassively, his only comment being: "A short life and a merry one—" though, since most of his short life had been spent hiding or running away, I find it difficult to concur with his opinion of merriment.

Now while Rurik was playing pinochle in the death house, there came to him a certain Father Jellusik who said that Dr. Holliday, the eye surgeon, wanted Rurik's eyes. The condemned man, laughing heartily, said: "Listen, Father, the D.A. offers me my *life* if I sing where the dough is stashed! And now somebody wants my eyes. No disrespect, Father, but don't make me laugh. D'you think I never heard how you can see things in a dead man's eye?"

Father Jellusik said, "My son, that's an old wives' tale. I have it on reliable authority that a dead man's eye is no more revealing than an unloaded camera."

Rurik began, "Once I looked into . . . well, anyway, *I* never saw nothing. What do they want my eyes for?"

"An eye," said Father Jellusik, "is nothing but a certain arrangement of body tissue. Put it like this: you are *you*, Rurik. If one of your fingers were chopped off, would you still be Rurik?"

"Who else?"

"Without your arms and legs, who would you be?"

"Rurik."

"Now say you had an expensive miniature camera, and were making your will. Wouldn't you give it away?"

"To the cops, no."

"But to an innocent child?"

"I guess I might."

"And the eye, you know, is nothing but a camera."

In the end Rurik signed a document bequeathing his eyes to Dr. Holliday, for the benefit of this remarkable surgeon's child patients, many of whom had been born blind. "You can't take 'em with you," Rurik is alleged to have said; thereby letting loose a tidal wave of emotion. One would have thought that Rurik was the first person ever to utter this proposition. The sob sisters took him to their bosoms, and put into his mouth all kinds of scrapbook philosophy, such as: "If more folks thought more about more folks, the world—" et cetera, et cetera. His last words, which were: "Hold it, I changed my mind," were reported as: "I feel kind of at peace now." The general public completely ignored the fact that there was a little matter of two and a half million dollars which Rurik had, to all practical intents and purposes, taken with him.

The few that thought of the matter said: "They'll track that money down. It's got to be somewhere, and they'll trace it. The FBI will throw out a net." But in point of fact, Little Dominic and MacGinnis being dead, no one had a clue to its whereabouts. It was buried treasure.

For years previous to the execution of Rurik Duncan, Dr. Holliday had been performing fabulous feats of eye surgery. To him the grafting of corneal tissue from the eye of a man recently dead to the eye of a living child was a routine affair which he regarded much as a tailor regards the stitching of a collar—good sewing was essential, as a matter of course, but the thing had to fit. And, somewhat like certain fierce tailors of the old school, he was at once savagely possessive, devilishly proud and bitterly contemptuous of the craft to which he was married. I know an old tailor who never tired of sneering at himself, who would have nothing to do with his fellow craftsmen because they were, in his opinion, mere tailors; but who ordered King Edward VII to get out of his shop and stay out, because His Majesty questioned the hang of a sleeve. Dr. Holliday was a man of this character—dissatisfied, arbitrary, unsatisfying, ill-natured, impossible to please. He had something like a contemptuous familiarity with the marvelous mechanism of the human eye, but would allow nobody but himself to talk lightly of it. He became famous when he grafted his first cornea. When the reporters came to interview him he appeared to be angry with the world for admiring him.

Irritable, disdainful, his face set in a look of intense distaste, and talking in an overemphasized reedy voice, he could make the most casual remark offensive. Reminded of his services to humanity, Dr. Holliday said, "Human eyes, sheep's eyes—they are all one to me. As eyes, a fly's eyes are far more remarkable.

Your eye is nothing but a makeshift arrangement for receiving light rays upon a sensitive surface. A camera with an automatic shutter, and damned inefficient at that. They do better in the factories. I have repaired a camera. Well?"

A reporter said, "But you've restored sight, Dr. Holliday. A camera can't *see* without an eye behind it."

Dr. Holliday snapped, "Neither can an eye see, as anybody but an absolute fool must know."

"Well, you can't see without your eyes," another reporter said.

"You can't see with them," said Dr. Holliday. "Even if I had the time to explain to you the difference between looking and seeing, you have not the power to understand me; and even if you had, how would you convey what you understood to the louts who buy your journal? Let it be sufficient for me to say, therefore, that the grafting of a cornea, to one who knows how to do it, is probably less difficult than an invisible darning job done to hide a cigarette burn in your trousers. Vision comes from *behind* the eye."

One of the reporters who wrote up things like viruses and astronomy for the Sunday supplement said: "Optic nerve—" at which Dr. Holliday swooped at him like a sparrow hawk.

"What do *you* know about the optic nerve, if I may ask? Oh, I love these popular scientists, I love them! Optic nerve. That's all there is to it, isn't it? A wiring job, so to speak, eh? Plug it in, switch it on, turn a knob—is that the idea? Splice it, like a rope, eh? My dear sir, you know nothing about the tiniest and most insignificant nerve in your body, let alone how it is motivated—and neither do I, and neither does anybody else. But you will suck on your scientific jargon, just as a weaning baby sucks on an unhygienic rubber pacifier. It is an impertinence, sir, to talk so glibly to me! 'Optic nerve'—as if I were a chorus girl! Can you name me thirty parts, say, of the mere eye—just name them—that you talk with such facility of optic nerves? Have you considered the extraordinary complexity of the optic nerve? The microscopic complications of cellular tissues and blood vessels?"

The reporter, abashed, said, "I'm sorry, Dr. Holliday. I was only going to ask if it might be possible—I don't mean in our time, but some time—really to graft a whole eye and, as you put it, splice an optic nerve?"

In his disagreeable way, unconsciously mocking the hesitancy of the reporter's voice—this was another of his unpleasant mannerisms—Dr. Holliday said, "Yes sir, and no sir. One thing is impossible and that is to predict what may or may not be surgically possible or impossible in our time. But I can tell you this, sir, as expert to expert: it is about as possible to graft a whole eye as it might be to graft a whole head. As every schoolboy must know, nervous tissue does not regenerate itself in the vertebrate, except in the case of the salamander in whom the regenerative process remains a mystery."

A lady reporter asked, "Aren't salamanders those lizards that are supposed to live in fire, or something?"

Dr. Holliday started to snap but, meeting the wide gaze of this young woman, liked her irises and, gently for him, explained, "The salamander resembles a lizard but it is an amphibian, with a long tail. An amphibian lives both in and out of water. Have you never seen a salamander? I'll show you one . . ." And he led the way to an air-conditioned room that smelled somewhat of dead vegetation, through which ran a miniature river bordered with mud. In this mud languid little animals stirred.

A man from the south said, "Heck, they're mud-eels!"

At him Dr. Holliday curled a lip, saying, "Same thing."

The Sunday supplement man said, "Dr. Holliday, may I ask whether you are studying the metabolic processes of the salamander with a view to their application—"

"No, you may not."

The lady reporter said, "I think they're cute. Where can I get one?"

Majestically, Dr. Holliday called to an assistant: "Everington, put a couple of salamanders in a jar for the lady!"

Next day there were photographs of a salamander in the papers, and headlines like this:

HEAD GRAFT NEXT?
MYSTERY OF SALAMANDER

After that Dr. Holliday would not speak to anybody connected with the press and was dragged into the limelight again only when he grafted the right eye of Rurik into the head of a four-year-old boy named Dicky Aldous, son of Richard Aldous, a wealthy paint manufacturer of Greenwich, Connecticut.

It was not one operation, but eight, over a period of about six weeks, during which time the child's eye was kept half-in and half-out of a certain fluid which Dr. Holliday has refused to discuss. The Sunday supplement writer, the "sensationalist," has hinted that this stuff is derived from the lizard-like amphibian salamander which, alone among vertebrates, has the power to regenerate nervous tissue. It is not for me to express an opinion in this matter. Only I will insist that sensationalists all too often are right.

Jules Verne was a sensationalist; and now we are discussing man-powered rockets to the moon. H.G. Wells was a sensationalist; but there really are such things as heavier-than-air aircraft, automatic sights and atomic bombs. I, for one, refuse to discount the surmises of the Sunday supplement man who put it as a conjecture that Dr. Holliday was using, as a regenerative principle, some hormone extracted from the humble salamander. Why not? Alexander Fleming found penicillin in the mold on lemon rind. Believe me, if it were not for such cranks, medicine would still be witch-doctoring, and brain surgery a hole in the head to let the devils out.

Anyway, Dr. Holliday grafted Rurik Duncan's right eye into the head of the four-year-old Dicky Aldous. It is not true that the father, Richard Aldous, paid Dr. Holliday a hundred thousand dollars for the operation; Mr. Aldous donated this sum, and more, to the Holliday Foundation, of which every schoolboy has heard.

To state the facts baldly: when the bandages were lifted, Dicky Aldous, born blind, could see out of his new right eye. The left remained sightless; but with the right the child could clearly discriminate objects. The lady reporter made quite a piece out of his first recognition of the color blue.

The Sunday supplement man, in whose bosom still rankled Dr. Holliday's rudeness, wrote an article suggesting that the delicate tissues of the human eye might be seriously altered by the tremendous shock of electrocution which, since it involves the entire nervous system, necessarily affects the optic nerve.

Dr. Holliday, after a few outbursts, became silent. It was noted that he was frequently found to be in consultation with the English brain specialist, Mr. Donne, and Dr. Felsen, the neurologist. Paragraph by paragraph the case of Dicky Aldous dropped out of the papers.

It was simply taken for granted that it was possible to graft a living eye. Other matters came up to occupy our attention—Russia, the hydrogen bomb, Israel, the World Series—and the fly-trap of the public mind closed upon and digested what once it had gapingly received as "The Dicky Aldous Miracle."

But this is far from being the end of the story. As an old friend of Richard Aldous and his family I was privileged to witness subsequent events. And since, now, it can do no harm and might do some good, I feel that I have the right to offer the public a brief account of these events.

Richard Aldous was a third-generation millionaire; genteel, sensitive, a collector of engravings. His wife, whom he had met in Lucca, was an Italian princess—finely engraved herself, and almost fanatically fastidious. Tourists used to wonder how it was possible for a sensitive, highbred Italian aristocrat to live in a *palazzo* surrounded with filth. Actually there is nothing to wonder at—the explanation is in the three wise monkeys, procurable at any novelty store. See no evil, speak no evil, hear no evil—and there you are, divorced from humanity. In extreme cases stop your nose, having previously sprinkled yourself with strong perfume.

As you can imagine, therefore, little Dicky Aldous in his fifth year was a child who was being brought up by his mother in complete ignorance of the ugliness that exists in the world. The servants in the Aldous house had been selected rather than simply employed—examined, as it were, through a magnifying glass—generally imported from Europe, expense being no object. Dicky's nurse was a sweet-natured English gentlewoman. From her he could have heard nothing but old-fashioned nursery songs—sung off-key, perhaps, but kindly and innocuous—and no story more dangerous than the one about the pig that wouldn't jump over the stile. The housekeeper was from Lucca; she had followed her mistress six years previous, with her husband, the butler. Neither of them could speak more than two or three phrases in English. Mrs. Aldous's maid, Beatrice, also was an Italian girl, a wonderful needlewoman and hairdresser but totally ignorant of the English language. Indeed, she seldom spoke any language at all—she preferred to sing, which the little boy liked, being blind.

Here were no evil communications to corrupt the good manners of poor Dicky Aldous.

Yet one day, about a month after the sensational success of Dr. Holliday's operation had been fully established, the English nurse came down from the nursery to make the required announcement that Master Dicky was asleep, and there was something in her manner which made the father ask, "Anything wrong, Miss Williams?"

Rachel Williams, the English nanny, didn't like to say, but at last she burst out—that somebody must have been teaching little Dicky to use bad language. She could not imagine who might be responsible. Closely pressed, she spelled out a word or two—she could not defile her tongue by uttering them whole—and Aldous began to laugh. "Tell me now, Miss Williams, what is the name of Mrs. Aldous's maid?"

"Beatrice," said Miss Williams, pronouncing the name in the Italian style.

"And what's the diminutive? How does Mrs. Aldous generally address her?"

"Bici," said the nurse.

"When Dicky first saw the light, bless his heart, where did you tell him it came from?"

"Why, Mr. Aldous, from the sun."

"Work it out, Miss Williams, and I think you'll arrive at the origins of most of this so-called 'bad' language."

All the same, when the nurse was at supper, Mr. Aldous went to the nursery where his son lay sleeping. On the way into the room he met his wife hurrying out, evidently on the verge of tears. She said, "Oh Richard, our boy is possessed by a devil! He just said, in his sleep, 'For crying out roud, cease, you rousy sandwich!' Where did he ever hear a word like 'cease'?"

Her husband sent her to bed, saying, "Why, darling, little Dicky has had to suffer the impact of too many new sensations, too suddenly. The shock must be something like the shock of being born. Rest, sweetheart." Then he went into the nursery and sat by the child's crib.

After a little while, stirring uneasily in his sleep, speaking in the accents of the gutters of the West, Dicky Aldous said quite clearly, "Ah, shup! Aina kina guya rat!"—distinguishable to his father as: 'Ah, shut up! I ain't the kind of guy to rat!'

Then, tossing feverishly from side to side and talking through his milk teeth, his face curiously distorted so that he spoke almost without moving his lips, Dicky Aldous said, in baby talk with which I will not trouble your eyes or distract your attention by writing it phonetically: ". . . Listen, and get it right, this time, you son-of-a . . ." He added a string of expletives which, coming from him, were indescribably shocking. Perhaps horrifying is the better word because you can understand shock, being aware of its cause; but horror makes no sense. That is why it is horrible—there lies the quintessence of nightmare, in the truth divorced from reason.

Typically, the first thing Richard Aldous thought of was Henry James and "The Turn of the Screw." How could this innocent child be saying words he could not possibly have heard in his tiny life? Now Mr. Aldous began to suspect the doctors, who are notoriously loose of language off the record among themselves. But presently, in a tense whisper, while the entire face of the child seemed to age and alter, Dicky said, "Dom, you take the big .45; Mac, take the cut-down, snub-nose, blue-barrel .38. What for? Because I'm telling you. A big gun looks five times bigger on a runt like Little Dominic. Get me? And a blue belly-gun looks twice as dangerous in the mitt of a big lug like Mac. Me, I take the Luger, because one look at a Luger, you know it's made for business. . . . But empty, I want 'em empty. . . . C'mon, let's have a look at that magazine, Dom. . . . Mac, break me them barrels. . . . Good! . . . You got an argument, Dom? Okay, so have I. I ain't got no ambition to graduate to be Number One, and in Montana, brother, they hang you up. . . . Okay, okay, call it unscientific, but you'll do as I say; because, believe me, this job'll be pulled using those things just for show. My weapon is time. Cease, Dominic. . . . Gimme a feel of that .45. Empty. Good, let it stay like that. . . . Okay, then, I want this straight, I want this right from the start. We'll go over this again. . . ."

Then Dicky Aldous stopped talking. His face reassumed its proper contours, and he slept peacefully.

Mr. Aldous met Miss Williams on the stairs. "It's worrying me to death," she said. "I cannot for the life of me imagine where Dicky-darling picked up the word 'cease.'"

Mr. Aldous said, "I think, just for a few nights, Miss Williams, I'll sleep in his room."

And so Mr. Aldous did. To be accurate, he lay down on the nurse's bed, and stayed awake, listening. He made careful notes of what poor Dicky said in his sleep—and many of the things the child said were concerned with visual memory, which the boy could not have had, since he was born blind.

". . . They's a whole knot o' cottonmouths on the island past Miller's Bend. What'll you give me if I show you? What, you never seen a cottonmouth? Give me something and I'll show you. It's a snake, see, a great big poison snake, and it's got a mouth like it's full of cotton, and poison teeth longer'n your finger. C'mon, give me what you got and I'll show you the cottonmouths," Dicky said, his voice growing uglier. ". . . What d'you mean, you ain't got nothing? You been wasting my time? Ever learn the Indian twist, so you can break a growed man's elbow? All right, boy, I'll show you for free. . . . Oh, that hurts, does it? Too bad. A bit more pressure and it'll hurt you for keeps—like *that*. . . . You still ain't got nothing to see the cottonmouths all tangled in a knot? . . . Oh, you'll get it, will you? You'd better. And you owe me an extra dime for learning you the Indian twist. . . . No sir, just for wasting my time I ain't going to show you them cottonmouths today—not till you bring me twenty cents, you punk, you. And then maybe I'll show you that nest o' diamond back rattlesnakes at Geranium Creek. But if you don't deliver, Malachi Westbrook—mind me now—I'll show you the Seminole jaw-grip. That takes a man's head clear off. And I'll show it to you good, Malachi. Yes sir, me and Teddy Pinchbeck will sure show you good! Mind me, now; meet me and Teddy Pinchbeck at the old Washington boathouse eight o'clock tomorrow morning, and bring Charley Greengrass with you. He better have twenty cents with him, too, or else. . . ."

Mr. Aldous wrote all this down. At about three o'clock in the morning Dicky said, "Okay, kids. You paid up. You're okay. Okay, I'll just borrow Three-Finger Mike's little old boat, and Teddy Pinchbeck and me'll take you and Charley Greengrass to look at them cottonmouths. Only see here, you kids, me and Teddy Pinchbeck got to pole you way past Burnt Swamp, and all the way to Miller's Bend. That'll cost 'em, won't it, Teddy? . . . You ain't got it? Get it. And stop crying—it makes me nervous, don't it, Teddy? And when I'm nervous I'm liable to show you the Indian hip-grip, so you'll never walk again as long as you live. You mind me now! . . ."

Dicky said no more that night. At about nine o'clock in the morning Mr. Aldous made an appointment with a psychologist, one Dr. Asher who, finding himself caught on the horns of this dilemma—*carte blanche* and an insoluble problem—double-talked himself into one of those psychiatric serials that are longer than human patience. But what was Dr. Asher to say? Little Dicky Aldous had no vision to remember with;

there was nothing in his head upon which juvenile imagination might conceivably fall back.

It was by sheer accident that Mr. Aldous met a lieutenant of detectives named Neetsfoot to whom he confided the matter, hoping against hope, simply because Neetsfoot had worked on the Rurik Duncan case.

The detective said, "That's very strange, Mr. Aldous. Let's have it all over again."

"I have it written down verbatim, Lieutenant."

"I'd be grateful if you'd let me make a copy, Mr. Aldous. And look—I have children of my own. My boy has had polio, in fact, and I've kind of got the habit of talking to kids without upsetting them. Would you have any objection—this is unofficial—would you have any objection to my talking to your son a little bit?"

"What in the world for?" asked Mr. Aldous.

Lieutenant Neetsfoot said, "Mr. Aldous, if you haven't got a clue to something, well, that's that. In that case, if you see what I mean, it doesn't even come within range of being understood. At a certain point you stop trying to understand it. Now sometimes something that makes absolutely no sense at all, flapping about in the dark, throws a switch. And there you've got a mystery."

"I don't get what you're driving at, Lieutenant."

"Neither do I, Mr. Aldous. But I'll give you the leading points, if you like. *A*—I know all there is to know about Rurik Duncan; saw him electrocuted, in fact. And a miserable show he made of it. *B*—I don't like to dig these matters up, but your son, five years old and born blind, had one of Rurik's eyes grafted into his head by Dr. Holliday. And now, *C*—the child is going word for word and point by point into details of things that happened about sixteen years before he was born and two thousand miles away!"

"Oh no, surely not!" cried Mr. Aldous.

"Oh yes, surely so," said the Lieutenant. "And geographically accurate, at that. What's more remarkable, your son has got the names right of people that were never heard of and who died before he was born. What d'you make of that? Teddy Pinchbeck was shot in a fight outside a church it must be ten, eleven years ago. A bad boy, that one. And where did I get my information? From Malachi Westbrook—he's a realtor, now. There *was* an old Washington boathouse, and Malachi Westbrook's the man that tore it down to make space for Westbrook Landing. Charley Greengrass runs his late father's store. There *was* a Three-Finger Mike, but he just disappeared. There really *is* a Cottonmouth Island just past a Miller's Bend, and in the mating season it's one writhing mass. And Rurik Duncan *did* break Malachi Westbrook's arm, before your son was born. Well?"

"This I do not understand," said Richard Aldous.

"Me neither. Mind if I sit with the boy a bit?"

"No, Lieutenant, no . . . but how on earth could he know about cottonmouths? He never saw one. He never saw anything, poor child. To be frank with you, neither my wife nor I have ever seen a cottonmouth snake. I simply don't get it."

"Then you don't mind?"

"Go ahead by all means, Lieutenant," said Mr. Aldous.

Neetsfoot went ahead—in other words, he sacrificed two weeks of his vacation in a dead silence, listening by Dicky's bed while the child slept. Mrs. Aldous was in the grip of a nervous breakdown, so that her husband was present only half the time. But he bears witness—and so, at a later date, does an official stenographer—to what Dicky Aldous said, in what was eventually termed his "delirium."

First, the child struggled left and right. It appeared to the detective that he was somehow trying to writhe away from something; that he was in the clutch of a nightmare. His temperature went up to 103 degrees, and then he said, "Look. This is the setup, you kids. The Pan keeps the engine running. Get that right from the start, Pan. Little Joe sticks a toothpick under the bell-push. I put the heat on. Okay? Okay!"

Lieutenant Neetsfoot knew what to make of this. The man who was called The Pan on account of his rigid face was driver for several gangsters; Little Joe Ricardo was a sort of assistant gunman who was trying to make the grade with the big mobs. The heat, as Neetsfoot construed it, was put on a union leader named M'Turk, for whose murder Rurik Duncan was tried but acquitted for lack of evidence.

M'Turk was shot down in his own doorway; the street was aroused less by the noise of the shot than by the constant ringing of M'Turk's doorbell, under which somebody had stuck a toothpick.

But all this had happened at least eight years before Dicky Aldous was born.

". . . And this I don't quite get," said Lieutenant Neetsfoot.

"There is something distinctly peculiar here," Mr. Aldous said. "But I won't have the child bothered."

"I'm not bothering the child, Mr. Aldous, the child's bothering me. Heaven's my judge, I haven't opened my mouth. Not even to smoke! The kid does all the talking, and Gregory takes it down on the machine. You can believe me when I tell you, there's something funny here. Your little boy has gone into details about the M'Turk shooting; and this I can't understand. Tell me, Mr. Aldous, do you remember the details of M'Turk?"

"No, I can't say I do, Lieutenant."

"Then how does the kid?"

"I must have told your people a thousand times: my son couldn't possibly have heard anything about the people or the events you keep harping on."

"I know he couldn't, Mr. Aldous. This is off the record and on my own time. That's understood, isn't it?"

"It is a most extraordinary situation, Lieutenant."

"You can say that again."

Mr. Aldous said, with a kind of detached enthusiasm that somehow disgusted the detective, "You know what? The eye of this man Rurik Duncan having been grafted, complete with optic nerve, it's almost as if the child's actually seeing through Rurik Duncan's optic nerve!"

"Almost as if," said the lieutenant.

"But *how?*"

"Ask the doctor, don't ask me."

And Dr. Holliday was, indeed, the fourth witness to the last, and most important, utterances of the boy into whose orbit he had grafted the right eye of Rurik Duncan. It happened, as previously, between two and three o'clock in the morning.

Dicky said, "Now listen. You, Dom, listen. And you listen, Mac. . . . You heard it before? Then hear it again. This is the way I want it, and this is the way it's going to be. Dom, you always were trigger-happy. First, no loads in the rods. I want these guns ice-cold. One thing I won't do, and that's hang. And in Montana they hang you on a rope. Never forget that. . . . Second, follow my timing, and you can't go wrong. We beat the lights. Remember, it's two million and a half in small bills. Better men than you have died for less. My uncle Gabe died through getting bitten in the leg by a hog. This way's more fun. . . . Third, the short haul in the armored truck, and the swift stash in the Rocks, you know where. Got it? Fourth, the quick scatter. Now somebody could get hurt. So let's get this right. Okay? I'll go over it again—"

At this point, Mr. Aldous, carried away by sheer excitement, cried, "Yes, but *exactly where* is the money? Where did we put it?"

Dicky sneered in his sleep, "And exactly where d'you get that '*did*'? It ain't put there yet. . . . And who's '*we*'? Little Dom and Mac I told already. There ain't no more '*we*.' Go burn me, mister, and sniff for it. . . . *We*, crysakes! Well, I guess you *got* to be dumb, or you wouldn't be a cop. Okay. You want to know where the dough is? I'll tell you. It's in Montana. Got that wrote down? Montana. It's going to be loaded in a great big armored track in Butte. And then where?—" The child laughed in a singularly ugly way. "It'll be my pleasure to tell you, mister: somewhere in Montana. All you got to do when I stash this dough is, scratch. Okay, Mr. Dickins?"

"Wasn't Dickins the name of the district attorney who offered Rurik Duncan his life if he would divulge the whereabouts of the stolen money?" whispered Mr. Aldous.

Lieutenant Neetsfoot replied, not without bitterness, "Yes, it was. For God's sake, shut up—I think you've already talked us out of that two and a half million. And here *I've* sat like a stone for fifteen days, and right at the end you must bust in and open your damn yap."

Deeply hurt, Mr. Aldous said, "My son has always responded to my voice."

The lieutenant looked at him with disdain, and then said, in a carefully controlled voice, "Yes, Mr. Aldous. Your son has always responded to your voice, Mr. Aldous. But damn it, that wasn't your son who was talking—that was Rurik Duncan! That was Rurik Duncan running over orders with Little Dominic and MacGinnis before the truck was snatched and the money stashed away! I told you to keep quiet like me, I begged you to keep your mouth shut like I did. But no, your son has always responded to your voice. Congratulations, Mr. Aldous; you've got the costliest voice in the world—it's just talked us out of ten per cent of two million six hundred thousand dollars!"

They sat by the crib until dawn but, his fever past, Dicky Aldous, perspiring freely, talked no more in his sleep.

When he awoke, his father, who had an unshakable faith in the power of his voice to arouse response in his hitherto blind son, said, "Now, Dicky-darling, tell Daddy-dear about Montana."

"Want to see blue," said Dicky; and became engrossed in the color and the shape of a large red non-poisonous nylon teddy bear of which he had previously known only the texture.

And from that day to this he has not talked of Montana. His memory of events preceding Dr. Holliday's operation is rapidly fading. Dr. Holliday, who visits the house from time to time, has put forward a half-hearted theory that, by some unexplained process, the regenerated nervous tissue, heavily charged with electricity, retained and conveyed the visual memory of Rurik Duncan only while this tissue was knitting. It may come back, he says, in adult life; or, on the other hand, it may not.

Lieutenant Neetsfoot, whom Mr. Aldous regards as a "character" pays a visit every other Sunday. He likes to play with the little boy. It was he who said to me, "This is unofficial, off the record; but I'm pretty observant. When I was a rookie I learned to watch you without seeming to. And I can tell you, there's something very, very funny about that kid's eye when he thinks he isn't being observed. He's seven now. I'm due to retire nine years from now. Call me crazy, but believe me—when that kid is old enough to have a car of his own and take a vacation without anybody else along, wherever he goes I'll follow him."

Here, for the time being, the matter rests.

RECENT AND FORTHCOMING TITLES FROM VALANCOURT BOOKS

Michael Arlen	Hell! said the Duchess
R. C. Ashby	He Arrived at Dusk
Frank Baker	The Birds
H. E. Bates	Fair Stood the Wind for France
Walter Baxter	Look Down in Mercy
Charles Beaumont	The Hunger and Other Stories
David Benedictus	The Fourth of June
Paul Binding	Harmonica's Bridegroom
Charles Birkin	The Smell of Evil
John Blackburn	A Scent of New-Mown Hay
	Broken Boy
	Blue Octavo
	A Ring of Roses
	Children of the Night
	The Flame and the Wind
	Nothing but the Night
	Bury Him Darkly
	Our Lady of Pain
Thomas Blackburn	A Clip of Steel
	The Feast of the Wolf
Michael Blumlein	The Brains of Rats
John Braine	Room at the Top
	The Vodi
	Life at the Top
Michael Campbell	Lord Dismiss Us
Basil Copper	The Great White Space
	Necropolis
	The House of the Wolf
Hunter Davies	Body Charge
Jennifer Dawson	The Ha-Ha
Lord Dunsany	The Curse of the Wise Woman
A. E. Ellis	The Rack
Barry England	Figures in a Landscape
Ronald Fraser	Flower Phantoms
Michael Frayn	The Tin Men
	The Russian Interpreter
	Towards the End of the Morning
	A Very Private Life
	Sweet Dreams
Gillian Freeman	The Liberty Man

Gillian Freeman	The Leather Boys
	The Leader
Rodney Garland	The Heart in Exile
Stephen Gilbert	The Landslide
	Monkeyface
	The Burnaby Experiments
	Ratman's Notebooks
Martyn Goff	The Plaster Fabric
	The Youngest Director
Stephen Gregory	The Cormorant
	The Woodwitch
	The Blood of Angels
Alex Hamilton	Beam of Malice
Thomas Hinde	The Day the Call Came
Claude Houghton	Neighbours
	I Am Jonathan Scrivener
	This Was Ivor Trent
Fred Hoyle	The Black Cloud
Alan Judd	The Devil's Own Work
James Kennaway	The Mind Benders
	The Cost of Living Like This
Cyril Kersh	The Aggravations of Minnie Ashe
Gerald Kersh	Fowlers End
	Nightshade and Damnations
	Clock Without Hands
	Neither Man Nor Dog
	The Great Wash
Francis King	To the Dark Tower
	Never Again
	An Air That Kills
	The Dividing Stream
	The Dark Glasses
	The Man on the Rock
C.H.B. Kitchin	The Sensitive One
	Birthday Party
	Ten Pollitt Place
	The Book of Life
	A Short Walk in Williams Park
Hilda Lewis	The Witch and the Priest
John Lodwick	Brother Death
Kenneth Martin	Aubade
Robin Maugham	Behind the Mirror
Michael McDowell	The Amulet

Michael McDowell	The Elementals
Michael Nelson	Knock or Ring
	A Room in Chelsea Square
Beverley Nichols	Crazy Pavements
Oliver Onions	The Hand of Kornelius Voyt
Christopher Priest	The Affirmation
J.B. Priestley	Benighted
	The Doomsday Men
	The Other Place
	The Magicians
	Saturn Over the Water
	The Shapes of Sleep
	The Thirty-First of June
	Salt Is Leaving
Peter Prince	Play Things
Piers Paul Read	Monk Dawson
Forrest Reid	Brian Westby
	The Tom Barber Trilogy
	Denis Bracknel
Andrew Sinclair	The Raker
	Gog
	The Facts in the Case of E. A. Poe
David Storey	Radcliffe
	Pasmore
	Saville
Bernard Taylor	The Godsend
	Sweetheart, Sweetheart
Russell Thorndike	The Slype
	The Master of the Macabre
John Wain	Hurry on Down
	Strike the Father Dead
	The Smaller Sky
	A Winter in the Hills
Hugh Walpole	The Killer and the Slain
Keith Waterhouse	There is a Happy Land
	Billy Liar
	Jubb
	Billy Liar on the Moon
Colin Wilson	Ritual in the Dark
	Man Without a Shadow
	Necessary Doubt
	The Glass Cage
	The Philosopher's Stone
	The God of the Labyrinth

WHAT CRITICS ARE SAYING ABOUT VALANCOURT BOOKS

"Valancourt are doing a magnificent job in making these books not only available but—in many cases – known at all . . . these reprints are well chosen and well designed (often using the original dust jackets), and have excellent introductions."

Times Literary Supplement (London)

"Valancourt Books champions neglected but important works of fantastic, occult, decadent and gay literature. The press's Web site not only lists scores of titles but also explains why these often obscure books are still worth reading. . . . So if you're a real reader, one who looks beyond the bestseller list and the touted books of the moment, Valancourt's publications may be just what you're searching for."

MICHAEL DIRDA, *Washington Post*

"Valancourt Books are fast becoming my favorite publisher. They have made it their business, with considerable taste and integrity, to put back into print a considerable amount of work which has been in serious need of republication. If you ever felt there were gaps in your reading experience or are simply frustrated that you can't find enough good, substantial fiction in the shops or even online, then this is the publisher for you."

MICHAEL MOORCOCK

"The best resurrectionists since Burke and Hare!"

ANDREW SINCLAIR

TO LEARN MORE AND TO SEE A COMPLETE LIST OF AVAILABLE TITLES, VISIT US AT VALANCOURTBOOKS.COM

Lightning Source UK Ltd.
Milton Keynes UK
UKHW041855020519
341997UK00001B/163/P

9 781939 140098